Judy Christenberry

A TEXAS FAMILY REUNION

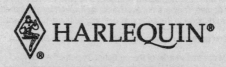

HARLEQUIN®

TORONTO • NEW YORK • LONDON
AMSTERDAM • PARIS • SYDNEY • HAMBURG
STOCKHOLM • ATHENS • TOKYO • MILAN • MADRID
PRAGUE • WARSAW • BUDAPEST • AUCKLAND

ISBN 0-373-75101-X

A TEXAS FAMILY REUNION

Copyright © 2006 by Judy Christenberry.

This edition published by arrangement with Harlequin Books S.A.

® and TM are trademarks of the publisher. Trademarks indicated with
® are registered in the United States Patent and Trademark Office, the
Canadian Trade Marks Office and in other countries.

www.eHarlequin.com

Printed in U.S.A.

Judy Christenberry's
CHILDREN OF TEXAS
miniseries includes:

Dear Reader,

I knew all along David would be the resistant one. It would be too much to expect every long-lost Barlow to *want* to be found. Poor David thought he already had enough family, but ultimately had to relearn what "family" really means. Who better to teach him than his blood siblings?

I think David's attitude is quite understandable— not everyone reacts well to change. We try to plan our lives and then when things change, we can be left floundering. That certainly has been true for me. My life hasn't turned out as I planned it long ago. In some ways it is so much better; in others, it's not so good. But I'm trying to make the best of what I have. David learns to do the same, and comes to love his old family while learning to relate to his new family. I hope you enjoy David's journey.

Since David is the last of the five living siblings, you may be wondering if I'm doing a ghost story with poor Wally. The answer is no, I don't write paranormal. The last book is about Vanessa, who has been in every book but hasn't had her own story. Since we all know she's firmly planted in the family camp, her story will be about what she does best—rescuing someone who also needs a family.

Thanks for your loyalty throughout this series. I love writing books about family, and I've enjoyed these stories especially. If you have any comments or questions, you can reach me at my Web site, www.judychristenberry.com.

Happy reading!

Judy Christenberry

ABOUT THE AUTHOR

Judy Christenberry has been writing romances for over fifteen years because she loves happy endings as much as her readers do. A former French teacher, Judy now devotes herself to writing full-time. She hopes readers have as much fun with her stories as she does. She spends her spare time reading, watching her favorite sports teams and keeping track of her two daughters. Judy lives in Texas.

Books by Judy Christenberry

HARLEQUIN AMERICAN ROMANCE
817—THE GREAT TEXAS WEDDING BARGAIN†
842—THE $10,000,000 TEXAS WEDDING†
853—PATCHWORK FAMILY
867—RENT A MILLIONAIRE GROOM
878—STRUCK BY THE TEXAS MATCHMAKERS†
885—RANDALL PRIDE*
901—TRIPLET SECRET BABIES
918—RANDALL RICHES*
930—RANDALL HONOR*
950—RANDALL WEDDING*
969—SAVED BY A TEXAS-SIZED WEDDING†
1000—A RANDALL RETURNS*
1033—REBECCA'S LITTLE SECRET**
1058—RACHEL'S COWBOY**
1073—A SOLIDER'S RETURN**

*Brides for Brothers
†Tots for Texans
**Children of Texas

Chapter One

Will Greenfield was enjoying the quiet solitude of the office one afternoon in February. The winds were blowing outside and the temperature hovered just below freezing. The weak winter sun struggled to make a difference, but it wasn't succeeding.

When he heard the outer door of Greenfield and Associates open, he looked up to see if his partners, Jim and Carrie Barlow, were returning. She'd had a doctor's appointment this morning, and Jim had gone with her. But the man who'd opened the door wasn't anyone he'd met before.

"Hello," Will said. He stood and walked around his desk and into the outer office. "I'm Will Greenfield. How can I help you?"

The man looked familiar, although Will was certain they had never met before.

"I'm not a potential client, Mr. Greenfield," the man said. "I'm here to see what kind of operation you run."

Will stared at the man probably twenty-five years his junior. "And why would you be interested in that if you're not a potential client?"

"My cousin is going to be working for you," he said tersely.

Will knew immediately to whom he was referring. "You're Alexandra Buford's cousin?"

"Yes. My name is David Buford."

"Does Alexandra have doubts about coming to work here?" Will asked.

"No, but I wanted to be sure you were legitimate."

"I see," Will said slowly. He had recently decided to hire a new agent when Carrie had become pregnant. Carrie wouldn't quit work completely, but she'd have to slow down a little.

"What kind of clients do you handle?"

"We do mostly insurance work. Occasionally we search for people or handle cases the police have given up on."

The man crossed his arms over his chest, and again Will was struck with a feeling of familiarity.

"Do you do any divorce cases, things like that?"

"Normally, no. Why? Do you have something against divorce cases?"

"They seem rather unsavory to me."

"What do you do for a living, Mr. Buford?" Will asked.

"I own a software company, Buford Works."

"And Alexandra didn't want to work for you?"

"No. She liked working in law enforcement, but she was tired of working the crazy hours. She doesn't have much seniority, so it would be a while before she could work days."

"So she said," Will said, watching the man.

"Is this a one-man office, just you and Alexandra?"

"No, I have two partners who aren't in today."

"Will she be the only woman?" David Buford asked sharply.

"No. One of my partners is female."

"Oh, good."

"Yes," Will agreed, still watching him closely.

"I won't take up any more of your time, then. Oh, I'd appreciate it if you wouldn't tell Alex I was here. She doesn't—" He broke off as the door behind him opened.

"David!" Alexandra Buford exclaimed, obviously surprised. "What are you doing here?"

"I just wanted to see where you'd be working, Alex. You know, check out the working conditions, the parking, that kind of thing," her cousin said.

Alexandra turned to her new boss. "Did he say anything to you to make you think I didn't want to work for you, Will? Because I can assure you I do want this job."

Will smiled as he noted the flash of anger in her brown eyes. "Don't worry, Alexandra. I didn't think you'd changed your mind."

"Good! So you can go now, David, now that you've checked out the *parking* at my new job."

"If you haven't started work yet," he said, "why don't I take you to lunch?"

"No, I don't have time. I want to set up my desk so I'll be ready to start," the young woman protested.

"You might as well accept his offer, Alexandra," Will said. "Your desk hasn't arrived yet. They called and told us it would be a couple of hours before it comes." He smiled at David Buford.

"Then why don't we eat at a restaurant near here so you can get back quickly," Buford suggested to his cousin.

"I guess so," the young woman said grudgingly.

"I apologize for interrupting your work, Mr. Greenfield," David Buford said, reaching out to shake Will's hand.

"No problem. I'm glad to have met you. Stop by anytime."

Once they'd left, Will sat back down at his desk and tried to return to work, but something about the man— or was it his name?—continued to puzzle him.

Will kept musing, searching his memory. Was the name Buford in any of the cases they were working on? It was funny that Alexandra's name hadn't struck him as familiar when he'd interviewed her. So why did it when it was attached to her cousin?

He was just getting up to search through a few files

when the office door opened again and his partners, Jim and Carrie Barlow, entered the office.

Will hurried around his desk to greet them. He hugged Carrie and shook Jim's hand, asking, "What did the doctor say?"

"He said I'm fine, and there's no reason I should sit at home on a pillow all day," Carrie said, rolling her eyes at her husband.

"I'm glad to hear it. I want you to train Alexandra so she'll be ready to take over when you're on maternity leave."

"It shouldn't take long," Carrie said. "After all, she's a police officer, or was."

"That's true," Will agreed.

Jim frowned. "I thought she was coming in this morning to get set up?"

"The desk was delayed, so she went out to lunch with her cousin."

Jim nodded. "Any messages?"

"Yes, that lady you phoned in Longview called back. She left another number where she could be reached during the day."

"Terrific. I'm hoping to get the name of the people who adopted David from her. She used to be a neighbor of my family's." Jim retrieved the message from his desk. "If you'll excuse me," he muttered, and dialed the number.

"He can't wait to find David," Carrie murmured to Will. "Did anything else happen while we were gone?"

"Well, Alexandra's cousin appeared. He wanted to see what kind of a company she was going to work for."

"That's sweet. I'm glad she has family who look out for her."

"I don't think she really needs to be looked out for, Carrie. She was a police officer."

"I know, Will. I just think it's nice. I was worried because she said she was an only child."

"Well, now you don't have to worry," Will said, and gave Carrie a quick hug. "I have to get back to work now." He disappeared into his office.

Carrie smiled and slid into the chair behind her desk. She turned on the computer and began to input the files she'd been working on. She'd become so involved in her work she didn't realize her husband had gotten off the phone until he spoke to her. "Yes, dear?"

"I said, that's strange."

"What?"

"The family who adopted David has the same last name as Alexandra."

"Really? But Buford isn't that unusual a name, is it?" Carrie asked.

"No, I suppose not. Maybe it's just one of those crazy coincidences."

"So does the family still live in Longview?"

"No. The lady isn't sure where they moved. She said they left Longview about three years after my parents' deaths."

"Alexandra's from here, isn't she?"

"Plano, she said," Jim muttered, naming a northern suburb of Dallas.

"What are you doing?"

"I just thought I'd look in the phone directory to see if there were any David Bufords listed in the area." He picked up the phone again and dialed a number, then asked the person who answered if a family named Buford had moved from Longview ten or twelve years ago.

When he hung up, Carrie asked, "Well?"

"Nope."

"Do you have more numbers?"

"Yeah. Are you willing to help make the calls?" He sent her a teasing look.

"You know I am, sweetheart, but I won't interfere if you want to make them all yourself."

"No, it doesn't have to be me who finds him, as long as we find him." He wrote down some numbers and brought them over to her desk.

After receiving a kiss from her husband, Carrie, too, began to dial the numbers he'd given her and to ask questions. Neither of them was having much luck when Will came out of his office again.

"What are you doing?" Will asked.

Jim explained what he'd learned.

"Buford is David's name now?" Will asked. Then he slapped his forehead with his hand. "I just met him!"

Both his partners stared at him.

"Who?" Jim asked.

"Your brother. It's got to be him. I thought he looked like someone I know. It was you!"

"Was his name Buford?" Carrie asked.

"Yeah. He introduced himself as Alexandra's cousin, David Buford."

"Where did he go?" Jim demanded, excitement in his voice.

"He took Alexandra out to lunch. They should be back soon, but I don't know if he'll come up with her. She didn't seem to appreciate his overprotectiveness."

Carrie grinned. "I know how she feels."

Jim scowled. "I don't overprotect you."

"Not by yourself. You and Will work together to protect me."

"Come on, sweetheart, you know we're only trying to make sure you're safe," Jim said.

She ignored him. "Did he really look like Jim?"

"Yes, he did. He isn't quite as tall, but he's still over six feet. His hair is dark, like all the Barlows, but he has blue eyes."

"My dad had blue eyes. Mom had brown," Jim said.

Just then Alexandra entered the office.

"Where's your cousin?" Will asked.

"I sent him back to work. I'm really so embarrassed that he came here checking up on my workplace."

Jim stepped forward. "Alexandra, was your cousin adopted?"

"Why, yes. How did you know?"

"We think he may be my long-lost brother. He was adopted by a family named Buford in Longview twenty-three years ago. He was five years old. They moved from Longview about three years later."

Alexandra stared at Jim. "The times fit. His family lived in Longview and moved to Plano about the time of my fifth birthday."

"Can you call him and get him to come back?" Jim asked.

"Yes, of course, but—"

"Don't tell him why, if you don't mind."

"Yes, but—"

"You could tell him you left your purse in his car," Carrie suggested.

"Oh, no, he'd check before he came back. I'll just tell him I need to talk to him." She pulled out a cell phone and quickly dialed a number. "David, where are you?"

After a pause she said, "Because I need you to come back. I need to talk to you. No, I can't explain on the phone."

Another pause. "Okay. Thank you."

She looked up at Jim. "He'll be here in fifteen minutes."

"Thank you. If he's my brother, we'll be reunited for the first time in twenty-three years."

"Now that I look at you, I guess David does resemble you a little. But he has blue eyes."

"Our father had blue eyes."

"Oh."

"Why did they move to Plano?"

"My father had started a company up here and he offered his brother a job when he'd lost his in Longview. So my uncle moved his family to Plano."

"What happened to the company?" Carrie asked.

"Oh, after college, David took it over. My father had died and Uncle Joe tried to keep it going, but he wasn't a very good businessman. David is a near genius. Since he took over the company, he's quadrupled sales, and earnings have gone up significantly. David has made a small fortune for our mothers. They now live comfortably together."

"Good for David," Jim said with a smile.

"We can't be absolutely sure he's your brother, Jim," Alexandra hurriedly said. "But they did live in Longview."

"I know. We'll see when he gets here." Jim turned to Will. "Did you mention my name to him?"

"No. He asked if I was the only member of the firm, and I told him I had two partners, but I didn't mention you by name."

"Will he remember his former family name?" Carrie asked. "I mean, he was only five."

"I think he will," Jim said quietly. "If he's shut out those memories, we'll help him to remember who he really is."

"Should you call Vanessa?" Carrie asked.

"Not until I'm sure. I don't want to get her hopes up. Or Rebecca's, either. We can plan a get-together once we know for sure."

Alexandra said softly, "It seems strange to think of David belonging to another family."

"It doesn't mean he won't still be a member of *your* family, Alexandra," Jim replied. "It just means his family will have expanded."

"If he does turn out to be your brother, how many brothers and sisters does he have?" she asked.

"There were six of us. Wally, the second oldest, died overseas. We were both in the marines. And I have three sisters, Rachel and Rebecca—twins—and Vanessa, the baby of the family. Vanessa is Will's stepdaughter."

"In the Buford family," Alexandra said, "he has two sisters and me, his cousin. Gives him quite a big family altogether, doesn't it?"

"We won't know if David is Jim's brother until we meet him," Carrie reminded her.

"I know, but—"

Alexandra was interrupted by the sound of someone coming up the stairs, and they all turned to the door.

David Buford entered the room, his gaze seeking out Alexandra. He didn't relax until he saw that she was okay.

Jim stared at his baby brother, his eyes tearing up. He no longer had any doubts.

Carrie stepped forward, holding out her hand. "Hello. I'm Carrie Barlow, one of Will's partners. This is my husband, Jim Barlow."

They all saw something flicker in David's eyes, but he lowered his gaze and extended his hand to Jim. "David Buford, Alexandra's cousin."

He looked at Alexandra. "You wanted to talk to me?"

"Actually, Jim wanted to talk to you, David. Do you recognize him?"

Not looking at Jim, he replied, "No, I don't."

Silence fell. Then Jim said, "We know you were adopted, David. What was your name before your adoption?"

"I don't remember," he said. "I'm sure you'll forgive me if I ask what gives you the right to ask me such a personal question."

"Nothing to forgive," Jim said, "but I believe you're my younger brother, David Barlow, who was adopted by a family named Buford after our parents were killed in a car accident twenty-three years ago."

"I don't think so," David said, turning away.

"Is your birthday August twentieth?" Jim asked.

"No! I have to go."

"Yes, it is, David!" Alexandra exclaimed. "Why are you lying to Jim?"

"I'm not lying!" David snapped. "I...all right, my birthday is August twentieth. But I'm sure there are a million other people born on that date."

"Yes, but how many of them are named David Buford?" Jim asked.

"Probably no more than three or four," David muttered, staring at the floor.

"Oh, David, coincidences don't happen *that* often," Alexandra exclaimed.

"Why not? We've already had one coincidence, haven't we?"

When Jim would've spoken, Carrie touched his arm. Then she said, "David, you're the last of the long-lost six Barlow children. Did you know that?"

He looked up first at Carrie and then at Jim. "You've found everyone but me?" he asked.

"Wally died overseas as a marine," Jim said softly. "Our sisters—Rebecca and Rachel, the twins, and Vanessa—have all reconnected. Vanessa was adopted by Vivian and Herbert Shaw. After Herbert died, Vivian hired Will Greenfield to find her daughter's siblings. Rebecca was living in Arkansas. Rachel was here in Dallas. Now she lives in West Texas."

David looked up at Jim and then quickly turned away, blinking rapidly as if trying to stop the tears. "I see. Perhaps I am David Barlow, your long-lost brother. I knew my name was Barlow but I didn't think anyone was looking for me."

"Is that why you denied being David Barlow?" Jim asked, frowning.

"Partly. I certainly don't want my mother upset. I owe her and Dad a great deal for rescuing me."

"And you think it would upset her for you to be reunited with your biological brother and sisters?" Carrie asked.

"Yes, I do. She's dependent on me for her income and well-being. My sisters depend on me, too."

"Yes," Alexandra said, shaking her head. "Your mother raised you to be the big brother her daughters didn't have. You were always taught to take care of everything for them. Too much, in *my* opinion."

"You're exaggerating, Alex! Mother doesn't make that many demands."

"You know I'm right," Alexandra insisted.

"Look," Jim said with amusement, "I don't want to cut short your argument, but, David, I'd like to arrange a meeting between you and our sisters. Would you object to that?"

"If we can do it quietly. I don't want Mom to know." David shrugged. "I know that sounds strange, but I really do owe her, the whole family, in fact, everything."

"Of course. I understand," Jim said. "If you'll give me your number, I'll call you when I've got something set up."

David reached in his suit jacket and pulled out a business card. "Here's my number at work. Give me a call there, if you don't mind."

"Of course not. Are you usually free on weekends?"

"Better if it's a workday night. I spend a lot of weekends at my mother's."

"I'm sure we can arrange something," Jim said. He reached out his hand. "I'm glad to see you again, David."

David stared at Jim's hand. After a minute he took it in his and let his gaze meet Jim's. "I'm glad to see you again, too."

Jim pulled David into an awkward embrace. Then David broke free and hurried out of the office.

Alexandra shook her head sadly. "I can't believe he did that!"

"What?" Carrie asked.

"Denied he was Jim's brother until he was forced to admit it. Then he asked Jim not to let his mother know about his other family."

"Would she be upset?" Jim asked.

"Oh, yes! She'll probably throw a fit. Ever since her husband died, she's clung to David, and she wouldn't want anyone coming between them. But he knew, when he heard your name. And he denied it!" Alexandra exclaimed.

"Don't be too hard on him," Jim said softly. "He might not have made it if your aunt hadn't adopted him when she did. David was the youngest of the boys and therefore the most vulnerable."

"How old were you?"

"We were five and eight," Jim admitted.

"Wow…you were very young too," Alexandra said.

"I guess." Jim grinned wryly.

"Jim's a big brother to the world," Carrie said as she slid an arm around her husband's waist.

"Well, I think David's lucky, he just doesn't know it yet," Alexandra said.

Chapter Two

Alexandra couldn't get the scene out of her mind, of Jim confronting David and trying to get him to admit his kinship. She'd worried about David for some time now. Because he had assumed both his father's and his uncle's responsibilities she feared he might be overloaded.

Not that David listened to her. He'd been raised to think a woman couldn't take care of herself or think for herself. His mother played the role of the southern belle to the nth degree. Her own mother was that way, too, but Alexandra had always been determined not to follow the same path.

Which explained her career choice; law enforcement was not for hothouse flowers.

"Do you want us to call you Alexandra or Alex?" Carrie asked as she carried over some supplies to Alexandra's new desk.

"It doesn't matter. I answer to both," she said with a smile.

"I noticed David calls you Alex," Carrie said.

"Yes. I was five when I first met him. He thought that because I was a girl, I would be easily dismissed, but I was determined to show him otherwise. I was in my tomboy phase. Maybe I still am."

"And he hasn't noticed you're a beautiful woman now?" Carrie asked, raising her brows.

Alexandra felt her cheeks flush. "I'm not beautiful, Carrie. But I do have a boyfriend."

"Well, I think you're very attractive, and I'm glad someone appreciates you. Is he a policeman?"

"Yes, he is. That was another reason I left my job as a cop. They frown on fraternizing."

"So you've made plans to marry?"

"Not yet, but I think… I hope my leaving will make things better." Alexandra smiled, thinking of her boyfriend. Neil had been one of her instructors at the police academy. After she'd finished the course and been assigned nights, he'd asked her out to dinner. They'd begun seeing each other when they could, but her schedule didn't fit well with his.

She was seeing him tonight. As far as she knew, he didn't know about her change of job. It had happened quickly while Neil was on vacation. He'd gone to Tennessee to see his family.

"You'll have to invite him to visit us. I'd love to meet him," Carrie said.

"I haven't even introduced him to my family yet. My

cousins are gorgeous," Alexandra said. "I don't want him to be…distracted."

Carrie chuckled. "Well, I can't wait to introduce you to Vanessa, Will's stepdaughter and Jim's sister. Also the twins, Rebecca and Rachel. They're all beauties, and you kind of have their look."

"Well, if it helps me do my job, that's all I care about."

Carrie perched on top of Alexandra's new desk. "I think it *will* help you. Men normally are not suspicious of pretty women." She grinned. "Anyway, I'm glad you're joining us. Will and Jim can be a little protective, but they do let you do your job."

"Will said you're pregnant. Are you going to keep working after your baby is born?"

"Yes. I'll take a couple of months off and then come back gradually. We have enough work now to keep *four* of us busy, so it may get a little rushed when I'm out of the office."

"That's okay. Will said we work as a team here, and that's one of the things that attracted me to this job. I work well on my own, too."

"You come with high recommendations from your sergeant."

Alexandra actually blushed. "He's an old friend of my father's."

"Whatever the reason, he sure thinks the world of you," Carrie said with a laugh. She pushed herself off Alexandra's desk. "If you need anything else, let me know."

"Thank you, Carrie. I appreciate your friendliness."

"We're like a family, Alexandra. I think you'll enjoy it here."

Alexandra watched the pretty blonde walk back to her own desk. Carrie and her husband seemed to have a loving relationship. Alexandra hoped that was true. They were such nice people.

She'd been impressed with Will, too, and had looked forward to starting her new job. Of course, she should've known David wouldn't believe she knew what she was doing.

From the moment her cousins had moved to Plano and settled just a few blocks away, she'd fought David for control. Since he was three years older, it wasn't exactly a fair fight. And her girl cousins had followed David around, doing whatever he told them to do. She'd tried to free the girls from his will, persuade them that he wasn't their boss, until the oldest cousin, Janet, had asked why they would want to do the opposite of what David said. He only had their best interests at heart. Their mother had said so.

Alexandra had immediately asked her own mother why they would want David to tell them what to do. Her mother had explained that some women preferred that men guide their decisions.

Alexandra was repulsed by such an idea. Her father always called her his little radical, even at five. She abandoned the effort on her cousins' behalf, but she refused to allow David to control her life.

"Alexandra," Jim said from his desk, "I've talked to my sisters, Vanessa and Rebecca, who live in Dallas. They're very anxious to meet David, but I've talked them into waiting until next Monday night. That way Rebecca's twin, Rachel, who lives in West Texas, will have time to get here."

Alexandra nodded. "Sounds good, but I'm not sure David will continue to associate with you and your sisters."

"Why not?"

"You heard David talk about his mother. He always tries to do whatever she wants. She only has to say she might like something and David finds a way to get it for her. He made a deathbed promise to his father to take care of his mother and sisters."

"You can't fault him for that," Jim said, frowning.

Carrie joined the conversation. "I agree with Alexandra. Being protective is one thing, but taking away choices stifles a person's development."

"But David just tries to grant his mother's wishes," Jim protested.

"But how can she appreciate what she gets if she never has to lift a finger to get it?" Carrie argued.

"Maybe his mother is too old to learn new tricks, sweetheart. Anyway, it's not our business. So we're all agreed next Monday night would be a good time to have my sisters and David meet?" Jim asked.

"Yes," Alexandra confirmed.

WHEN DAVID GOT BACK to his office, he found one of his best employees waiting for him.

"Hi, Pete. What's up?" he asked as he took off his jacket and settled behind his desk.

Pete Dansky shut the office door and moved closer to David's desk. "We've got problems."

David's head snapped up. "What are you talking about?"

"Our government contact just called me. He said we must have a spy, because someone else submitted a bid very close to ours in design."

"That can happen," David said slowly. "Did it have—"

"It had everything ours had except for the last bit of work you and I did. I described it to Williams and he told me it wasn't there."

"Then we still have a chance?" David asked.

"Yes, as long as the last bit doesn't get passed on."

"Are those papers in your office?"

"They're in my safe!"

"Good. But we can't let anyone work on them but you and me, and that's going to slow things down. Can we meet the deadline?"

"I don't think so. Even if you and I work day and night, I doubt we can finish."

"So we have to find who betrayed us and fast." David leaned back in his chair, closing his eyes.

A long minute passed. At last Pete said, "David? Are you napping or thinking?"

"I'm thinking. I need to make a phone call to some people who can help us."

"You're sure?"

"Yes. It's a detective agency that my cousin works for. I'll see if they can take our case and how soon."

"And you think they'll be able to find the spy?"

"Yeah, I do. What I need you to do, Pete, is list all the employees who had access to the files."

"Okay. I'll be back with a list in ten minutes."

"Good."

Once Pete had left his office, David got the number of Greenfield and Associates and dialed it. When a woman answered who wasn't his cousin, he assumed it was Carrie.

"This is David Buford. I need to know if your firm does personnel reviews."

"Yes, David, we do. What have you got in mind?"

He explained the situation.

"I see. Let me pass you to Jim. Hang on."

It was a couple of minutes before Jim picked up the line. "David, Carrie explained your situation and what you want. I think we can do the job, assuming we have complete access to your employee files and are allowed to interview anyone we want. I've got a few things I can put off. We can start tomorrow morning. Does that work for you?"

David told him it did, and they hung up. He felt satisfied. He might not've seen Jim for twenty-three years, but he sensed that Jim hadn't changed. He'd been honest as a boy, and he still was. David could trust his older brother.

THE NEXT MORNING Jim was sitting in David's reception area when he arrived. Which was good. What wasn't good was that Alex was sitting next to him.

"What's she doing here?" he demanded when he saw his cousin.

Jim raised one eyebrow. "She works with us now, remember?"

"Of course, but yesterday was her first day. Isn't she kind of green?"

Jim rose to his feet. "Suppose the three of us go into your office, David," Jim suggested. "We can discuss things there." Alexandra stood up, too, her face flushed with anger.

David led the way into his office. After they followed him in, he closed the door. "Well?"

"Look," Jim said, "we didn't hire Alexandra to train from scratch. We hired her because she's already been trained in most things. She's quite able to do an interview and assess the data in the files. If you have a problem with that, you'll have to hire another firm."

Alexandra protested. "No, I don't want you to lose—"

Jim stopped her. "This is not your decision, Alexandra. The four of us discussed it yesterday and decided this would be our approach. It's up to David to decide whether or not to accept what we're offering." He stared at David.

"Of course. I just thought…" David said. "Your wife seemed…."

"Carrie is the one who suggested Alexandra come. Alexandra has done a lot more interviews than Carrie."

"You have?" David asked, frowning at his cousin.

"Of course I have, David. That's a big part of a cop's job, talking to people, either as victims or criminals."

"Oh, yeah. Well, that's fine. I didn't mean to make a fuss. It just took me by surprise."

"So you're satisfied?" Jim asked.

"Yes, of course. We thought you could work in the conference room next door, unless you need separate rooms?"

"No, we're going to work together. We'll look over the files and then start pulling people in to interview."

"Okay, sure. And I'll take you both to lunch."

"It would be better if you ordered in food for the three of us and anyone else you trust so we can discuss any questions we have."

"Oh, right. Yeah, Pete Dansky. We'll bring in lunch."

"Great. Then we'll see you in three hours," Jim said with a smile and moved to the door, Alexandra following.

EARLIER, JIM AND ALEXANDRA had discussed how they would handle the interviews. Jim had suggested they take turns being the lead, and Alexandra had said she felt comfortable with that. Once they were in the conference room, they each took two files and read them.

"Anything in either of yours?" Jim asked.

"No, they look fairly straightforward."

"Okay, let's interview these four, one after the other. You be the lead on your files and I'll be the lead on mine."

The four interviews were completed in only half an hour. Jim and Alexandra put those files aside and moved on to another four. When they had questions about something in a file, they called Carrie. She found the information online and reported back.

By noon, they had cleared twenty-four employees. When the last interview ended, David and another man came into the room, loaded down with packages of food.

"How'd the morning go?" David asked.

"So far, so good," Jim said. "You have some great people working for you."

"We only have a couple of questions," Alexandra said. "One person had actually worked for the company who made the duplicate bid. She hadn't listed it on her previous employments. Her name is Judith Green."

Both men stared at Alexandra.

"She did?" David asked. "And she told you that?"

"Alex noticed the time gap in her list of previous employers. Apparently, whoever interviewed her didn't ask the right questions."

"Maybe whoever it was was distracted by a pretty face," Alexandra challenged, staring at her cousin.

"It wasn't me!" David declared.

"It was me," the other man said. "I remember because I did notice the time gap in her résumé. I asked her and she said her mother had been sick and she took time off work to nurse her back to health."

Alex made some notes on her pad. "We'll check that out, Mr.—" She broke off since she hadn't been introduced to him.

"Oh, sorry," David said. "This is my right-hand man and best friend, Pete Dansky."

"Hello. I'm Alexandra Buford, and this is Jim Barlow."

Pete shook both their hands, but his gaze returned to Alexandra. "You have the same last name as David?"

"Yes, he's my cousin."

"That's right. He said his cousin worked for your company, but I thought—"

"Give them a chance to eat their lunch, Pete," David said hurriedly.

"Right. We brought in some cheeseburgers and fries." Pete began pulling out neatly wrapped packages. Soon they were all eating.

Jim asked, after taking a bite of his hamburger, "What does Miss Green do for the company?"

"She tests our new programs to be sure they work."

Jim exchanged a look with Alex. "I think we should get Carrie to do a check on her mother and that illness she had. She can do it while we continue our interviews." He pulled out a cell phone and hit a button, then proceeded to tell Carrie the details.

When he disconnected, he said, "My wife will check it out and let us know as soon as she can. Will can go out and get her some food. We're expecting our first child, and I trust him to take good care of her."

"Congratulations, Jim," David said in a stilted manner, drawing a curious look from Pete. Then he returned to business. "So what's the other question?" he asked. "Alex said you had a couple...."

Alexandra took over. "There was a man who had been fired by you and then rehired. About five years ago. He didn't seem to have an adequate explanation for that." She stared at David.

"Oh. That was Bill Bardwell. Yeah, he's okay. I fired him because he fell asleep at work several times. Then his wife came to see me. They'd had a baby and then she got sick, and he was taking care of her and the baby all night long. I apologized to him and rehired him."

Jim nodded and said, "The only decent thing to do." He took another bite of his cheeseburger and chewed.

"You and Alex seem to work well together," David said, watching Jim.

"Yes, we do," Alex said instantly, as if challenging him to prove differently.

"I just wondered...I mean, Alex is very...."

Jim grinned. "So's my wife. And she'd kill me if she thought I was hitting on Alex instead of doing my job. Your cousin is safe with me, David."

"That's a strange thing to accuse the man of," Pete protested.

"I just like to make sure," David snapped. He turned bright red and stood up suddenly. "Right. I'll be in my office if you have any other questions."

There was a stunned silence in the conference room after David's abrupt departure. Finally Pete rose to his feet. "I don't know why David's acting the way he is. It's not like him. He's a good man."

"I know he is, Pete, but thanks for saying that." Jim smiled at him.

"You say that like you've known him a long time."

Jim picked up a French fry, studying it, as he said, "I knew him when he was a lot younger."

"Oh, I didn't know that."

"It doesn't matter. I know he's concerned about Alex. He's just trying to protect her."

"I've told him I know what I'm doing," Alexandra said. "He doesn't want to believe it."

"Give him time, Alex. He seems to be dealing with a lot right now," Jim said. He stood and gathered up the remains of their lunch and threw it in the trash can.

Then he offered his hand to Pete. "Thanks for bringing us lunch and eating with us. We'll let you know as soon as we've figured it out."

"David and I will be waiting to hear from you," Pete said.

He left the conference room. Only minutes later, Jim's cell phone rang. It was Carrie.

Chapter Three

Carrie said that she'd talked with Judith Green's mother. She'd pretended to be a health insurance salesperson and Mrs. Green hadn't been interested in purchasing any. She'd said she'd never been sick a day in her life.

When Carrie had asked about any children, whether they might need health insurance, Mrs. Green had explained that her daughter worked for Carey & Co., and they had excellent insurance.

Carey & Co. was David's competitor.

"Well, that was a slam dunk," Jim said with a smile. "We'd better call her back, and call David and Pete in, too."

"I'll take care of it," Alex said as she stood. "We've finished faster than I thought we would."

She stopped by the secretary's desk and asked for Judith Green to be called. Then she walked to David's office door. It was open and she stuck her head in. "David?

We think we've found the leak. Do you and Pete want to sit in on the interview?"

"Already? You bet." He got up and followed Alex out, asking his secretary to call Pete to join them. The four of them were together before Judith arrived.

When the young woman came into the room and saw the four people sitting at the table, she paused and then took a chair. "You asked to see me again? Is there something I didn't tell you?"

Alexandra smiled. "Judith, Pete said you told him you hadn't worked the six months prior to taking this job because your mother was very sick."

"Yes, that's right," she agreed at once. "I didn't mention it this morning because I didn't realize it mattered."

"Normally, it wouldn't, but we've spoken to your mother and she denies ever being sick a day in her life."

"You spoke— She doesn't like to admit to being sick." Judith seemed a little more unsure of herself.

"She also said her daughter had excellent insurance with her employer."

"Yes, that's true. Our company has great insurance." She smiled at David.

"She said your employer was Carey & Co," Alex said.

Judith jumped to her feet. "No! No, she...made a mistake."

David spoke for the first time. "Judith, we'll give you the opportunity to resign at once, or we'll fire you and sue you for industrial espionage. Your choice."

DAVID WAS VERY PLEASED with the job Alex and Jim had done. He offered to take them to dinner to celebrate the successful conclusion.

"I can't," Alex said hurriedly. "I already have plans."

David wasn't sure he believed her. Then he turned to Jim. "How about you and Carrie join me and Pete for dinner?"

"Thanks, David, but we'll all be dining together on Monday of next week. Why don't we celebrate then?"

"Okay, that'll be fine. I do need to find someone else to replace Judith right away, I have to admit. We're under a deadline."

"Why not ask Susan?" Alex suggested. "She's taken courses in computers."

"No, I don't—" David began.

"Who's Susan?" Jim asked.

"My youngest sister," David replied.

"Relatives you trust can be good employees," Jim said.

Pete said, "I met her, but I didn't know she had any interest in computers."

"Yeah, well, my mother doesn't encourage her because she thinks it's not feminine to do computer work."

Alex cast Jim a wry look.

Pete said, "That's crazy. What's she doing for a job?"

"She's a salesclerk at a dress store," Alex said, "and she told me she doesn't like the work."

"Okay, okay, I'll call her," David agreed. "I'd better call Mom, too. Hopefully, she'll understand."

"Tell your mom the company needs Susan. That should help," Alex suggested.

"Yeah," David agreed. "Why don't you come with me to tell her about the job, Alex."

"I told you I had plans for the evening."

"Neil again, I suppose?" David asked unhappily.

"Yes," Alex replied. David didn't seem happy with her choice for a companion, but then he'd never been happy with the men she dated.

Jim said, "Thanks for the work, David, and I hope Susan takes the job, but we've got to get back to the office. I'll call you about next Monday night later in the week."

"Right, thanks, Jim."

Pete stood beside David as the other two left. "Is your mother really opposed to women working with computers? That's crazy."

"I know. Mom's that way."

"Want me to go with you to tell her?"

David smiled. "No, I'm a big boy. I can face her on my own. You can go with me to talk to Susan, though."

"Sure, good idea, since I'll be the one to train her. I can see if we'll work well together."

They set out for the dress store where Susan worked. When they entered the place, Susan was ringing up a sale. As soon as she'd finished, David asked her if she could take a break. She got approval from her supervisor and the three of them went to a small café next door.

Once they were seated and ordered drinks, David explained their problem. "We've got to find someone who knows computer software to fill a sudden vacancy at the firm. And I thought of you."

Susan's eyes opened wide with excitement. Then she slumped back in her seat. "I'd love it, but you know how Mom is. She'll be so upset if I—"

"I know, honey, but I think it's time you worried about making yourself happy rather than Mom."

"Wow, you sound like Alex," Susan said with a giggle.

"Maybe I do. I thought Mom would change with time, but she hasn't. Alex is right. You have the right to choose work you'll enjoy. Maybe it isn't in computers, but you'll never know until you try."

"You'll back me up?"

"I will."

"And I'll be the one to train you," Pete said, smiling warmly at Susan.

David shot a look at his best friend. Pete seemed really eager to train Susan. Taking a second look at his sister, he realized she was quite pretty. Hmm.

"Do you have to give notice to the store?"

"I think you're supposed to, but I'll tell my supervisor this is an emergency. It is, isn't it?" Susan asked.

"Absolutely!" Pete said.

"Yeah, Pete's right. It would be best if you came with us right now."

"Then let me talk to my supervisor. They've got plenty of help right now. I don't think my leaving will be a problem. Then I can follow you to the office and start this afternoon."

"Maybe I should wait for Susan and ride with her to the office, so she won't get lost," Pete suggested.

David told him that was good thinking, though he knew it was totally unnecessary. But Susan wasn't objecting, either.

He left them together and drove to his mother's home, which she shared with her sister-in-law—Aunt Gladys, Alex's mother.

"Mom, I need to talk to you," David announced after he'd entered the house. His mother and Gladys were sitting together knitting in front of the television.

"Yes, dear?"

"I've talked Susan into quitting her job and coming to work for the company."

That got his mother's attention. "What? Oh, no! I can't allow that! You should've talked to me first."

"I'm sorry, Mom, but Susan has a lot of training in computer work. I think she should be using it, not working in a dress store. She doesn't even *like* the job, according to Alex."

"Alex is always trying to talk her into being independent!" his mother snapped.

Gladys laughed. "That's my girl! Strong-minded as ever."

"Yes, she is, isn't she. She was at the office this morning, helping us find a spy. She and Jim interviewed and checked backgrounds and found out who had been passing our information on to the competitor. That's why we need Susan. If she doesn't like it, I'll help her find another job, Mom. I'll make sure she's happy."

"Who's this Jim?" his mother demanded.

"He works with Alex at Greenfield and Associates. They did a great job."

"Is Alex interested in him?" Gladys asked hopefully.

"No, I think she's dating a cop," he said casually.

"Oh! I didn't know. She never tells me anything."

"Well, if this Jim's not married," his mother said, "Alex could introduce him to Susan."

"He's married, Mom. Susan will find someone." His other sister, Janet, was married, and it seemed to be his mother's goal in life to marry off Susan.

"I had hoped you'd introduce Susan to someone, but you never have."

"I did try a few times, Mom, but it never worked out."

"Well, I don't like you hiring Susan to work for our company. She shouldn't have to work there."

"She thinks it might be fun to try, Mom. So can I tell her you don't mind?"

"I suppose. But if she doesn't like it, you must help her find a *nice* job at once."

"I promise, Mom."

Though his mother protested his leaving so quickly, he headed back to the office. He found Pete and Susan in Pete's office. He was already teaching her "Quality Assurance," which had been Judith's job.

"Everything going okay?" David asked.

The pair jumped as if they'd been doing something illegal.

"Oh, David, yes, everything's fine," Susan said. "Pete is doing a wonderful job of teaching me what to do. Did…did you talk to Mom?"

"I did, and she agrees, as long as I promise to find you another job if you don't like this one."

"Thanks, David," Susan said.

"No problem. Pete, everything okay with you?"

"Sure, everything's great," Pete answered, but his smile was directed to Susan, not David.

David made a mental note to keep an eye on his friend. He thought a lot of Pete and wouldn't mind having him in the family. In fact, he preferred Pete to his current brother-in-law, Janet's husband, Jerry. He worked in his father's stock brokerage firm and David found him pretentious and snobbish. But David's mother was very impressed with him.

Returning to his office, David sat for a moment to think. He knew Alex would approve of what he'd done today, though he hadn't done it for her approval. He'd been worrying about Susan for a while now. She hadn't seemed happy. Maybe now....

His thoughts turned to Alex. He'd always tried to be a big brother to her, too, since she had no brothers. His desire to protect her was what had prompted him to pay a visit to Greenfield and Associates.

Of course, she didn't appreciate his efforts. But she was working with Jim. She'd be okay. He wished he could say as much about her latest boyfriend. Neil Logan was a divorced cop and seven years older than Alex, who was only twenty-four, the same age as Susan.

He focused his mind on his work. He'd given enough time to thinking about his family today. Besides, thinking about the company was important to his family, since they enjoyed the proceeds.

ALEX WAS THRILLED. She'd just successfully completed her first case at her job, and tonight she'd get to tell Neil about her job change. Now if he was interested in a future with her, there was nothing to keep them apart.

She was in the kitchen when she heard Neil's knock on the door. They usually ate at her apartment since Neil said it would be better if they kept their relationship quiet. That was another reason for her leaving the police force. She wasn't comfortable with secrets.

When she opened the door, Neil swept her into his arms and kissed her. "Hey, did you miss me?" he asked.

"Of course I did." She smiled. He always wanted to

know if she'd missed him, even if it was only a day or two since she'd seen him. "How was your family?"

She listened patiently while he talked about his family. She was waiting for him to finish, hoping he would ask about what she'd done during his vacation. Dinner was over before he got to that stage. By then, Alex was more than a little irritated.

"So, what did you do while I was gone?" he finally asked.

"I got a new job," she said casually.

"You what?"

"I got a new job."

"You left the police force?" he asked, astounded. "You should've discussed it with me first!" His tone held anger.

Alex stared at him in disbelief. David had been concerned, but he hadn't acted like this. "Why? Don't you think I can make decisions for myself?"

"Of course I do, but I think I know what's best for you."

Why hadn't she noticed how controlling he was? He usually dominated the conversation, it was true, but she'd figured that was because he'd had more experience and thus, more to say. It seemed she'd been mistaken.

"Don't worry," he said. "I can probably pull some strings and get you back on the force."

"No, thank you," she said clearly.

"Yeah, I can talk to the sergeant and tell him you made a mistake and—"

"I don't want you to talk to the sergeant, and I didn't make a mistake!"

"Come on, Alex, I'm just trying to help. I don't want you working somewhere else."

"Doesn't it matter what *I* want?"

"Sure, baby, but we won't get to see each other as much."

"Why not? I won't be working nights, and it won't matter if someone sees us together if I'm not on the force."

"I don't think it would be a good idea for me to be seen with a quitter." Neil reared back in his chair, as if challenging her.

Suddenly Alex knew what she had to do. "You're probably right," she said.

He grinned at her. "I knew you'd come around. I'll talk to the—"

"No, I'm not agreeing to come back to the police force. I'm agreeing that I shouldn't be seen with you."

"So you want to keep our relationship a secret?"

"No. I want to end it."

"What are you talking about?" he roared.

"You heard me. I don't want to see you again." She stood and went to the door, holding it open.

"Come on, honey, you can't mean that."

An hour ago, she probably *wouldn't* have meant it, but now she saw Neil in a different light. He no longer had any authority over her. "Yes, I can. I've made a choice that I'm happy with, and I wouldn't want to embarrass you by being seen with you."

"But if we keep meeting here, no one will know."

"Hurry up and go, Neil. Bugs are getting in."

He stalked out of her apartment. "I had plans for us," he said from the doorway. "We could get married. We could have a couple of kids and you wouldn't have to work."

An hour ago that plan would've thrilled her. Thank goodness she'd woken up in time.

Before she could say anything else, Neil continued, "After all, you get money from the company your family owns. It's not like we'd be hard up."

"Goodbye, Neil."

"You think about it. Let me know when you come to your senses."

"Right." She closed the door in his face.

After he'd left, she plopped down on her sofa. She'd made the right decision; she had no doubt about that. But she hated that she'd wasted so much emotion and time on a man who wanted to control her and take advantage of her income.

She'd been a poor judge of character. Maybe it was because he was a higher rank on the force and had seemed so interested in her. She'd almost slept with him. She'd been tempted a couple of times, but something held her back.

Now she was glad she hadn't given in to momen-

tary urges. He was a handsome man, but underneath…
She wondered about his marriage and divorce. Maybe
his wife—

The phone rang.

"Hello?" she answered, fearing it was Neil.

"Alex? It's Susan. Have you heard my news?"

"No, I haven't. Tell me!"

"I'm now working for our company! David con-
vinced Mom I should try it and see if I like it. I can't
believe she agreed!"

"I can't, either, but I'm very happy for you."

"Oh, me, too. I spent the afternoon at the new job and
it's quite absorbing."

"I'm glad."

"And do you know the best part?" Susan asked.

"You get to work with David?"

"No! I get to work with Pete."

"Ah, he is cute, isn't he?"

"You've met him?" Susan asked in surprise.

"Yes, Jim and I worked at the company today to find
the spy."

"Oh, that's right. The spy was fired and that's why
they had an opening. I'm so glad you found her, because it got me out of that awful dress shop Mom
loves."

"I know. She and my mom go there all the time."

"Yeah. They haven't changed their style in twenty
years. Do you think we'll ever be like that?"

Alex chuckled. "I don't know. If not that, we'll probably have other faults that will drive our kids crazy. If we have kids."

"What's wrong?" Susan asked, picking up on Alex's depressed state. They'd been in the same grade in school from kindergarten on and had shared a lot of things. She knew her cousin well.

"Nothing," Alex said, not wanting to talk about breaking up with Neil just yet.

"Maybe I can talk Pete into taking me out to dinner and you and Neil could come with us!" Susan immediately suggested. "I'd love to meet him."

"Maybe David can double-date with you."

"Why not you and Neil?"

"I'm not going to be seeing him anymore."

"Oh, I'm sorry, Alex, I didn't know."

"It just happened tonight. I discovered that's he a control freak. He doesn't want me to make any decisions."

"Like Mom?"

"Worse. And he seemed to know about the income I get from the company, too. He wanted to live off it someday."

"Oh, that's horrible."

"Yeah. So maybe you can get Pete to take you out to celebrate your getting the new job."

"I'm having second thoughts. I mean, Pete's my boss. I guess I'll ask David. He'll probably tell me I shouldn't date him if he's my boss."

"It is something to think about, Suse. I mean, I was blinded by the fact that Neil had a higher rank than me."

"I will think about it. But I'm excited about the job. It's a new start for me."

"Yes, it is. I'm proud of you."

DAVID WAS WORKING at home. He had a condo near the office and worked most evenings. After all, he didn't have a social life.

He'd tried dating, and he'd discovered women liked to date wealthy men. He had a nice car, a nice home, had the title of president of his company. But they didn't like dating a workaholic. After his last girlfriend had complained about how boring he was, he'd given up dating.

He answered his phone after it rang, expecting it to be his mother. "Hello?"

"David, it's Susan. I just wanted to thank you again for my new job. I really enjoyed myself today."

"I'm glad, honey, but don't decide too quickly. Give yourself time to be sure."

"I will. Oh, and I like Pete, too."

"I'm glad."

Apparently Susan still had something to say, but she wasn't saying it. But she wasn't hanging up, either.

"Was there something you had a question about?"

"Um, yes. What is your policy about dating?"

It didn't take David long to figure out what his sister wanted to know. "You mean Pete?"

"Is he seeing someone right now?"

"No, I don't think so, but…well, you know Mom's kind of a snob, don't you?"

"You mean because she slobbers all over Jerry and his family because they've been members of the country club for generations? Yeah, I know. So?"

"Do you remember Pete's last name?"

"Dansky? What's wrong with it?"

"Nothing as far as I'm concerned. But his father came over from Eastern Europe when Pete was a little boy. He's a U.S. citizen now, but he wasn't born here."

"I don't care."

"But Mom would. I just wanted to point that out. Anyway, is Pete interested in you?"

"I don't know. I hope so. I thought you and I could go out and celebrate my new job and…and you could ask Pete to come."

"Were you going to ask Mom?"

"No, I just meant you and me and maybe Alex."

"Alex would probably have a date with that cop." David wasn't happy about that.

"I don't think so," Susan said.

That got David's attention. But Susan didn't elaborate, and he wasn't about to ask. Alex's love life was none of his business, was it?

Chapter Four

"Alex? I'm sorry to call so late but…."

"It's okay, David. I hadn't gone to bed."

"I need to talk to you about Susan. And I need to ask you for a favor. Can you spare me a night this week? I mean, without canceling a date with that cop?"

Alex drew a deep breath of relief. At first when David started his request, she feared Susan had told him about her breaking up with Neil. "Yes, I suppose I could save a night for you, if it's necessary."

"According to Susan, it is. She wants me to suggest we go out to celebrate her new job…and ask Pete to go with us to even out the numbers."

"Even out the numbers?"

"Ah, you see the problem. Susan and I are two, an even number. That's why we need you. That would make the numbers uneven and give us a reason to ask Pete to join us. Susan's kind of interested in him, but doesn't want to seem too forward at such an early stage."

"Why don't you ask one of your dates?"

"I've given up dating."

Alex frowned. "Why?"

"One of them explained that wealthy men were favorites unless they were workaholics. Then they were just boring. I'm a workaholic."

"Oh, David! That was stupid of her. You're not boring! You mustn't give up dating," Alex told him.

"Thanks, sweetheart, but for right now, I need you to be my date for Susan's plan to succeed. Okay?"

"All right. I don't mind helping Susan out."

"Good. How about tomorrow night?"

"All right."

After she hung up the phone, Alex thought about her younger years, when she'd tried to get David to notice her. He wasn't her real cousin, and she'd had a major crush on him. But he'd been much too busy to pay any attention to her—after all, she was more than three years his junior.

So she'd finally turned her attention to boys her own age and found them much more receptive. But she wasn't exactly booked up. She could go on this fake date as a favor to Susan.

As she was climbing into bed later that night, she realized she hadn't once thought of Neil since David had called. Maybe she hadn't gotten over that ridiculous crush, after all.

THE NEXT MORNING, both Will and Carrie congratulated her and Jim on their efficient job for David's company.

"Carrie, you did as much work as either Jim or me," Alex told her. "We all worked together so well."

"Yes, we did, didn't we?" Carrie agreed. "That just proves that we were smart to hire you."

"I hope so," Alex said. "What's on my plate for today?"

"Will wanted you to start work on this case," Carrie said, handing her a file. "It's for one of our insurance companies. If you have any questions about how to proceed after you've read the information, just ask me or Jim."

"Great, Carrie, thanks." Alex settled at her desk, thinking how much better this was than night duty as a cop.

Later that afternoon Alex was working on the computer, making notes on the man who was apparently trying to con the insurance company, when she got a call from David.

"What time do you get off work tonight?" he asked without preamble.

"We usually close at five," Alex said, lowering her voice. She didn't want the others to think that she was a clock watcher.

"So will you be ready if I pick you up at six-thirty?"

"That's not necessary. I can meet you somewhere."

"No, it will work better if I take you and Susan in my car. We're meeting Pete."

"Where are we going?"

"I thought we'd try Outback. Their steaks are good."

"So it's going to be a first-class celebration. Shall I offer to pay half?"

After a momentary pause, David said, "I think I can bankroll this evening, Alex. Any remarks like that would ruin the illusion Susan is trying to create."

"All right. I won't say anything like that. But I'll still be glad to—"

"Your job is to dress like you're going out on a date with the cop. Only you'll be with me!"

She was left holding a dead line. He'd hung up on her. Impossible man!

Did he think she wouldn't wear something nice just because she was going with him? Well, she'd show him. She'd wear that green knit dress that hugged her figure. And she'd wear her sexiest perfume, too. She didn't think he'd complain then!

"Alex?" Carrie called. "Is anything wrong?"

"No! Of course not. Why would you think that?"

"Because I can hear the dial tone all the way over here. You haven't hung up yet."

"Oh!" She replaced the receiver.

"Any problems?" Carrie asked again.

"No, it was just David yanking my chain, as usual."

"That's a family trait," Carrie said with a smile.

"Ha!" Alex exclaimed. "There are times when I'm glad he and I aren't really kin."

Carrie eyed her speculatively. "Well, I was very glad I wasn't kin to Jim when he arrived here."

"Oh, I didn't mean *that*," Alex said, blushing. "I did have a crush on him when we were kids, but I grew out of it."

When she left at five o'clock, she hurried straight home. She didn't have much time if David was going to pick her up at six-thirty. She was going to knock his socks off tonight.

DAVID HAD WONDERED if he could convince Pete that he and Alex were interested in each other. After all, Pete thought they were cousins. He hadn't told him he was adopted. But Pete hadn't had any problem with his story. David suspected he would've gone out with anyone as long as Susan was part of the group. But he wouldn't tell Susan that.

He picked her up first. He thought it would be better to have Susan with him before he picked up Alex. Susan suggested they all three go in one vehicle so she could accept a ride home with Pete if he asked her to.

"Want me to knock on Alex's door?" Susan asked.

"No, I'll go get her. You'd better get in the back seat if you're going to sell Pete on the idea that Alex and I are on a date." He got out from behind the wheel and walked up to the door of Alex's condo. After a rap on her door, he leaned against the wall, waiting. His experience was that women were usually late.

When the door opened at once, he was surprised. Stepping forward, intending to tell her he appreciated her punctuality, the intention fled his mind when he saw her.

David had realized Alex was beautiful when she began attracting boys. But he'd kept her at arm's length, still regarding her as a younger cousin. Through the years, she'd grown more and more beautiful—and more and more tied up with the latest man in her life.

Tonight, she was wearing a dress that clung to her curves, and the color, green, brought out the green in her hazel eyes and complemented her softly curling, shoulder-length auburn hair. "You look terrific, Alex," he said as he caught a whiff of a wonderful scent.

"Thank you," she said quietly, no triumph in her voice.

But he wouldn't have blamed her if she had been annoyed at him. He'd been rude to hang up on her that afternoon.

When they reached the car, Susan, too, complimented her cousin. "I wish I'd gotten some height from Dad, like you did from your dad, Alex. That kind of dress looks great on a tall person."

"Well, your family has all the computer skills, honey, and I think Pete really likes that," Alex said with a grin.

"Oh, great. I want to be loved for more than how I work a computer!"

David comforted his sister. "I don't think that's what got Pete's attention, brat."

"Don't you dare call me that in front of Pete," Susan protested.

He laughed. "I'll try not to, but it's your fault if I do. You and Janet were always pestering me."

"They were just doing their jobs. That's what all children are supposed to do for the oldest. Make his life hell." Alex grinned at David.

Susan laughed. Then, as they pulled into the restaurant parking lot, she asked, "What kind of car does Pete drive?"

David stiffened. "Are you so shallow that you have to know what a man drives before you decide if he's worth your time?"

"No! I just wondered if he was here already."

Her hurt tones reminded David that this was Susan, not Janet. "Sorry, honey. I must've gotten you confused with our sister."

"Oh, all right, I forgive you. So do you see his car?"

"Yes, I do. I bet he's inside waiting for us."

When he stopped the car, Susan was the first out. She smoothed down her hair and drew a deep breath. Alex stepped to her side. "You'll do fine, Suse."

Susan gave her a shy smile. "I hope so."

"Here we go," David said, stepping between the two ladies. He took each of their hands and moved toward the door of the restaurant. In the darkened interior, Pete was sitting on a bench, awaiting their arrival. He popped to his feet as they entered.

"Hi, Pete. You beat us here," David said, extending his hand to his friend. "You remember Alex, don't you?"

"Yes, of course, Alex, it's good to see you again," he said politely. Then he swung his gaze to Susan and his face lit up. "Hi, Susan."

"Hi, Pete," Susan said with the same enthusiasm.

David exchanged a look with Alex. Then he took her hand and followed the hostess to a booth for four. Standing back, he watched her slide gracefully into the booth.

Then he remembered to say, "I hope a booth is okay with you, Pete."

Pete, in the process of following Susan into the booth, said, "Oh, um, yeah, it's great."

Which seemed to describe the rest of the evening from Pete and Susan's point of view. They gazed into each other's eyes most of the evening, scarcely acknowledging David and Alex.

"Do you think they even know we're here?" Alex whispered to David at one point.

"Yeah, but I don't think they care," he replied.

"But how can Susan work for Pete? They'll never get anything done."

David murmured, "It's my job to make sure they do."

Out loud, Alex said, "My steak is really good. How about yours, David?"

"Yeah. But in honor of Susan's new job, I think we need to order a Chocolate Thunder from Down Under."

The other two were talking to each other, still oblivious to Alex and David.

"I suppose we could all share one," Alex agreed.

"Or maybe order two of them, one for each couple."

"So we can eat ours…then eat theirs before it melts?"

"Well, that's possible," David drawled. "But it happens to be Pete's favorite dessert."

"I'm not sure we're even necessary," Alex murmured.

"I thought we were. Pete's a little gun-shy."

"He is? Why?"

"Do you remember his last name?"

"Of course I do. It's Dansky."

"Well, some people are selective about who they call friend."

"As they should be," Alex said, a little puzzled.

"Pete fell for a woman from a wealthy family, though he didn't realize they were wealthy at the time. Her parents were appalled that she would even date a person with *that* kind of last name."

"You're kidding!" Alex exclaimed.

Pete looked up. "What? Did we miss something?"

"No, David was telling me something about my mother and my aunt," Alex said quickly. Then she muttered, "About my aunt at least."

"So, you understand," David said. Pete and Susan were back in their own world.

"Yes. That hadn't occurred to me when I met Pete. What does your mother think about him being a good friend?"

"She hasn't said, and I haven't asked her." David looked up as their waiter arrived at the table.

"Are you finished, ma'am, sir?"

"Yes, we're all finished," David said, gesturing to Pete and Susan, too.

"But they haven't—"

"You can take their plates, too," David said.

"I can put their food in takeaway boxes if—"

"No, thanks, but you can bring us two Chocolate Thunders from Down Under, though."

"Yes, sir, right away." The waiter took Pete's and Susan's plates from the table. They didn't object.

Five minutes later, just before the dessert was served, Susan tried to cut another piece of steak and realized her plate was gone. "What happened to our food?" she asked.

David grinned. "We got tired of waiting and ordered dessert. We told the waiter to take your plates away."

"Oh. Were we eating too slowly?" she asked.

Pete immediately apologized. "I'm sorry, Susan and I were…we were talking about work."

"It's nice that you have something in common," David said blandly.

Alex almost choked, and David helpfully pounded her back.

"Th-thank you, David!" she gasped. "Sorry, my drink went down the wrong way."

At that moment the two desserts arrived with four spoons.

"We thought two would be enough. These are meant to be shared." David picked up his spoon and pulled one of the desserts between him and Alex, leaving the other one to Pete and Susan.

"Perfect," Pete said as he picked up a spoon and handed it to Susan. "I love these," he added, looking into her eyes.

"Oh…I do, too."

David heard Alex's swiftly indrawn breath between those two comments. He squeezed her hand and offered her a bite of ice-cream-and-brownie out of his spoon.

She took the bite. "Thank you. Mmm, it's good."

He smiled. "Yeah, perfect ending to a perfect night."

"So my behavior didn't disappoint you?" Alex asked, raising one eyebrow.

"No, Alex, it didn't. I…and Susan, owe you one. Feel free to collect at any time." When she said nothing, he added, "I'll even explain to the cop why you went out with me."

He expected her to reject his offer, but with a laugh, she said, "Not necessary."

Her answer caught his attention. But he didn't ask her to explain. Not then. He would wait until he took her home.

ALEX KNEW she'd made a mistake.

She hadn't wanted to tell David about her breakup. Mainly because she felt like a fool, believing Neil had actually loved her. All he'd loved was himself.

Throughout the years, whenever she'd done something or made a decision to do something, she'd always checked out his reaction. She didn't want to see his reaction this time, though she was proud she'd chosen to end her relationship with Neil.

She was afraid he'd feel pity, and she didn't want his pity.

Continuing to eat the dessert long after she'd had enough, she avoided conversation. She wished she could catch a ride with Pete when it came time to leave. But she knew Susan would never forgive her if she tried such a thing.

David insisted on paying the bill, telling Pete it was a family celebration. Then he said, "But you could do me a favor."

"Sure, pal, anything."

"Well, it's kind of late, and I wondered if you could run Susan home. That way, we could all get home sooner."

Susan made a perfunctory protest, but Pete's eager willingness reassured her.

The other two sped out of the restaurant. David and Alex left in a more leisurely style.

"He certainly took the bait, didn't he?" Alex said.

Again David heard something in her voice. "You sound envious. That can't be true."

"Of course not," she said, warning herself to be more careful. "But I don't think we'll need to play this game again."

"Why do you say that?" David asked as he followed her out of the restaurant.

"Because Pete didn't seem the least resistant to Susan's charms. Unless you want to start a matchmaking firm, I'd guess we're out of the business." Alex tried to look happy.

"Yeah," David said. She hoped he really agreed.

They rode in silence to her condo. When he stopped the car, Alex said, "Thanks for the ride," and tried to open her car door.

But David had locked the door.

"The door won't open!" Alex said.

"I know," David said. "I want to know what's going on."

"I don't know what you're talking about."

"Have you and Neil broken up?"

Alex stared at him. "That's the first time you've ever used his name."

David shrugged.

"Why would you do that?" she asked.

"I think I feel a little sorry for him."

Alex glared at him. "No need."

"*Did* you break up with him?"

"That's none of your business!" She tried the door again, in frustration.

"Alex, I'm your cousin. I just want to know you're okay."

"I'm okay," she snapped. "I promise I'll let you know if I'm not."

"I thought you two were…serious."

"Only if I agreed to always be available to him, and, oh, by the way, cook dinner for him and share my income from the company. And, best of all, do everything he said."

"So you got rid of him? Because if you didn't, I'm going to."

Alex allowed a small smile at his answer. "No, it's not necessary for you to go to such extremes. I took care of him."

"Good. Then you won't mind helping me out again."

Chapter Five

"What? Why?" Alex demanded.

"I'm talking about Monday night." He gazed levelly at her, waiting for her to remember.

"Your family reunion? What do you want me to do about that?"

He gave her a crooked smile. "I want you to go with me."

When she would've answered, and he could tell the answer would be no, he held up a hand. "Wait, let me explain."

"Okay, I'm waiting."

"I'm embarrassed by how I acted when I met Jim and Carrie. It was wrong, but I'd just spent half the day with Mom. I panicked at the thought of having more family. I can barely take care of what I've got now."

"What did your mother want you to do?"

"She wanted me to leave the office and go work on the plumbing at Janet's home—after all, she said, I fixed *her* plumbing one day. When I asked her what was wrong with their plumbing, she said they wanted a bigger master bathroom. Nothing was wrong—they just wanted more. I told her I couldn't be spared and they could afford to hire a plumber."

"I'm sure she didn't understand."

"Of course not. It turns out that Jerry wouldn't spend the money and Janet was complaining about how hard she has it in her five-thousand-square-foot home."

"And your mom thought you were being selfish?" Alex guessed.

"Yeah. Even when I told her we were preparing a bid for a government project, which is why I needed Susan."

"You should've mentioned the magic words— decreased earnings."

"Couldn't she figure that out on her own?"

"Apparently not." Alex smiled at him. "Your mother has always thought the world revolved around her."

"She's not that bad."

"Yes, she is, and because of her, you insulted Jim."

"I didn't—at least, he didn't hold it against me, and I haven't even explained why." He drew a deep breath. "But that's why I need you to go with me. Besides, you already know Jim and Carrie and Will."

"So do you."

"Yeah, but they like you."

"David, you're being silly…but I'll go with you. Does that make you feel better?"

"Yeah. A lot better." He leaned over and kissed her cheek. Then he unlocked her door.

"CARRIE, WHAT TIME is David supposed to be at Will and Vivian's this evening?" Alex asked after she'd started to work Monday morning.

"Didn't Jim tell him? I'm sure we're having dinner at seven, which means the evening will begin about six or six-thirty so we can all visit together. Wait a minute and I'll call Vivian."

"I don't want to cause any trouble."

Carrie waved a dismissive hand toward Alex as she picked up the phone. A moment later she hung up. "Yes, Vivian said any time between six and six-thirty will be fine."

"Um, I should've told you before you called Vivian. David asked me to come with him. I hope that'll be all right."

"Of course it will be. Betty loves to have big parties."

"Who's Betty?"

"Oh, she's Vivian's housekeeper. She and her husband, Peter, have been with Vivian since the beginning of her first marriage. They're part of the family."

"They sound wonderful. You know that TV show with all the kids and a housekeeper that took care of them? I so wanted her in my family," Alex said with a laugh.

"Yeah, me, too. Only, with me, there was only me

and my parents. Then my dad died and there was just me and my mom."

"Like me. There's just me and my mom, too."

Carrie looked stricken as Jim came into the office. He immediately moved to his wife's side. "What's wrong, hon?"

"Nothing," Carrie said at once. "I was being silly."

"What did I say to upset you, Carrie?" Alex asked anxiously.

"I was thinking about my mom's death and how alone I felt then. If it hadn't been for Will…."

"I didn't know your mother died!" Alex exclaimed. "Oh, I'm so sorry, Carrie!"

Carrie pushed away from Jim's embrace, rubbing her forehead. "You didn't say anything wrong, Alex. I'm emotional right now. My hormones…."

"Your hormones are just fine, sweetheart," Jim assured her. "And now you have me and all the rest of the family. You're not alone and our child won't be alone, remember?"

Carrie smiled. "Yes, I remember." She reached up and kissed him briefly. "Now I need to get back to work."

"It's almost lunchtime," Jim announced. "How about I take two lovely ladies to lunch? What do you say?"

"Are you sure we can afford the time?" Carrie asked.

"I'm sure," Jim said, pulling her from her chair.

As they all stood, Will came through the door. "Hey, what's going on?"

"I'm taking the ladies to lunch. Want to come?"

"You bet. I wouldn't turn down that invitation."

Alex didn't know if Will had read Jim's mind, or there had been something in his voice, but she was glad Will confirmed their decision. She was sure it would be good for Carrie.

When they reached the restaurant, a casual place with TVs mounted in the corners, they all ordered, then sat waiting for their food.

"Will, I thought I should tell you that David asked me to come with him tonight. Is that okay?" Alex said.

"Of course it is. Actually, David called Vivian this morning to ask that same question. I'm delighted you're coming—you can get to know the family. Anyone who works for me becomes part of the family."

"That sounds lovely. And David will think so, too. He just…the other day, when he came to the office to check on me, he'd spent half the day with his mother, arguing, and he wasn't sure more family would be a good thing. That's why he was so…reluctant to admit he was Jim's brother." She went on to explain the details.

"Poor David," Jim said. "Maybe my not being adopted wasn't such a bad thing."

Carrie covered her husband's hand with hers. "Maybe not, but you were strong."

"I promise David is, too," said Alex. "But sometimes I think they adopted David to have someone else to take care of her. Her husband did everything for her."

"I know that kind of woman," Will said. "Thank goodness Viv isn't that way, in spite of her first husband, Herbert, trying to make her dependent on him."

"He couldn't convince Vanessa, either," Jim said with a grin.

"That's the truth!" Will agreed.

"But…isn't dependency on someone a good thing?" Alex asked, confused.

Carrie chuckled. "Of course it is, but when you try to *force* someone's dependence, it isn't. And if you're a parent with a rebellious son or daughter, you're in big trouble. A daughter like Vanessa, for instance—well, that girl doesn't follow the easiest road at times."

"Oh, I can't wait to meet her," Alex said with a laugh.

"Just think of Jim in a wig," Will said drolly.

"I think all my sisters are pretty independent," Jim added.

"That's true," Will said.

Just then the waiter brought their food. As they started eating, the talk turned to work. Alex had a few questions and found them easy to ask in such a relaxed setting.

They were getting ready to leave when a news brief came on the television. "This just in. Shots were fired at a Plano businessman this afternoon. While no one was injured, the police are trying to find the shooter."

Alex gave a low scream as she recognized the man talking to police. "That's David!"

"Damn, she's right!" Jim agreed. "I'm heading out there as soon as you can get me to my car, Will," Jim said.

"Should I go, too?" Alex asked.

"I think I can handle it, Alex, since we know David's okay. If he were hurt, I'd agree you should go."

When they reached the office five minutes later, Jim, after a hurried kiss for Carrie, said, "I'll be back as soon as I can." Then hopped out and got in his own car, peeling out of the parking lot before Will had managed to park his car.

"I hope he doesn't get a ticket before he gets to Plano," Will said.

"I'm sure he'll be fine, Will," Carrie said. "But he's just found David. He's not going to lose him now."

Alex, impressed that Jim felt that way in spite of David's rude behavior, knew the right person was on his way to David's side.

WHEN JIM REACHED David's building, he took the elevator up to the second floor where his office was located. Standing by the receptionist's desk was a uniformed policeman. Since his main occupation seemed to be flirting with the young woman, Jim started around him for David's door.

The man quickly stepped in his way and said, "Excuse me, sir, but do you have an appointment with Mr. Buford?"

"No, but I think he'll see me," Jim said.

"If you'll give his secretary your name, she'll ask."

"Of course. It's Jim Barlow."

The woman clicked on the intercom. "Mr. Buford, a Mr. Jim Barlow is here to see you."

"Send him in," came the voice through the intercom.

The policeman stepped back, and Jim opened the door to David's office. He immediately focused on David, who had several people in the office. Jim recognized Pete and shook his hand. He figured the other two men were detectives.

"I'm sorry, gentlemen, but my best guess is teenagers joyriding," David said.

"Not with thirty-eights," one of the detectives muttered.

"Thirty-eights?" Jim asked. "That sounds unusual, David."

"And who are you, sir?"

Before Jim could answer, David said, "This is my brother, Jim Barlow."

Pete's head snapped up and he stared at Jim. Jim looked at David with approval.

"Why don't you have the same last name?" the detective asked.

"We were orphaned as children when our parents died. I was young enough to be adopted, but Jim wasn't. We've only recently found each other."

"And how did you find out about the shooting, sir?"

"We were having lunch at a place with televisions.

Actually it was Alex who realized they were talking about you," Jim told David.

"Is she okay?" David asked. "I didn't think they would give my name on the news."

"They didn't, but they showed you talking to the police."

He sighed. "Well, at least Mom doesn't watch the noon news."

"And you can't think of anyone who might've had reason to shoot you?" the policeman asked again.

"Did you tell them about your competitor?" Jim asked.

"It couldn't have anything to do with that, Jim," David protested.

The police asked for details. Jim provided them, mentioning the spying that had gone on.

"Mr. Buford, did you press charges against the spy?"

"No, I threatened to if she made me fire her, but she quit, instead."

After the police finally left, Jim had a few more questions for his brother. "How much damage did they do?"

"They shot one of my tires and my back window completely out."

Jim frowned. "How far away were they?"

"Just a few yards."

"Either they're amateurs or they just wanted to scare you."

Pete spoke up. "Why would you say that?"

"Most guns for hire are excellent shots. At that distance, they should've been able to hit you, if that's what they intended."

David nodded slowly. "I'll admit that did occur to me. I figured they were either very bad at what they did, or I'd been very lucky."

"Yeah. So what now?"

"I had my car picked up to be fixed. I guess I'll get a rental for tonight."

"I've got a better idea," Jim said. "I'm not trying to sell you anything, but I think you need some security at your company. Why don't I take a look at your setup and see what I can recommend while you work this afternoon? Then I'll take you to the office and you can meet Alex there. She can take you to Will's house tonight and bring you home."

"That would be fine, but, Jim, I'm not sure we'll make any changes around here. I mean, that was probably just a random thing that won't be repeated."

"I understand, David, but in case it's not, you might think about your employees. If someone came after you here in the office, some of them might be hurt."

"I'll think about it. Just come back here when you're finished looking around. Jeannie will find me if I'm not in my office."

"Sure."

"I'll be interested in hearing your ideas, too, Jim," Pete said. "David needs protection, even if he doesn't realize it."

"I agree, Pete. Oh, and David, you might give Alex a call so she can relax before you start back to work."

Jim left David's office and after getting a notebook and pen from Jeannie, the receptionist, he headed for the first floor to begin his surveillance from the ground up.

ALEX, RELIEVED after a talk with David, got back to work. The only problem was she'd planned on driving to her condo in Plano and changing her clothes before she picked up David and returned to Highland Park for the evening. Will and Vivian lived in Highland Park, where their office was also located. The area was an exclusive city within Dallas that was about twenty-five minutes from her own condo. David offered to go by her home and pick up something for her, but since neither he nor Jim had a key, that wouldn't work.

"I don't know how you're fixed for money, Alex," Carrie said when Alex told her the situation, "but you could go shopping and buy something. I mean, Will won't mind if you take an hour or two off. And North Park, a big shopping mall, is just a few blocks away."

"Oh, I couldn't…just a few blocks? I could be back in under an hour, and I'll be staying late waiting for David. Do you really think that would be all right?"

"Of course it would, but you look fine. I should've said that first. You don't need to change clothes."

"I still want to change, though, and I could use a new

outfit," Alex said. "I wish you could come with me—
I'm not familiar with the stores in that mall."

"Wait a minute," Carrie said, and jumped up from her
chair. She walked to the door to Will's office. "Will,
Alex needs to take an hour off and do a quick shopping
trip for tonight. Is it all right if I go with her?"

"Sure. But she doesn't need to dress up for tonight,
if that's the problem."

"She knows, but it'll just make her feel better."

"Then go. I'll see you in a while."

"Thanks, Will." She turned to Alex. "I'm ready if
you are."

"Oh, I love this job!" Alex said with enthusiasm.

Carrie chuckled. "I'll remind you of that when you're
working overtime."

"Willingly, I promise."

When David arrived at the office late that afternoon
with Jim, Alex had changed into the silky dress she'd
bought for the evening. And the shoes she'd bought to
match it.

"Wow! You look great, Alex," David said.

Alex jumped up from her computer and hugged her
cousin. "Are you okay? What did the police say?"

"They said to be careful."

Alex looked over his shoulder at Jim, a question in
her gaze.

"Unfortunately, they didn't have a lot of information
for us," Jim said.

"I got a lot more from Jim," David said. "And if I believed such a thing would ever happen again, I'd do what he told me to do."

"Which was what?"

"Alex, it wasn't—"

"I want to hear what Jim told you," Alex said.

"I pointed out some security issues I thought he should address," Jim said with a smile. "But he's the one who has to make that decision."

"David! What's wrong with you? Why won't you tighten your security?"

"Alex, calm down. Take some deep breaths. It isn't necessary. The shooting was random. Jim admitted they probably weren't trying to kill me. If anything, they wanted to scare me."

"Well, they sure scared *me!*" she exclaimed.

"You're being ridiculous," he said, taking her by the shoulders. "I'm fine, and I'll continue to be fine. Did you wear this to work this morning?"

"You're trying to distract me," Alex claimed.

"Yeah, is it working?" David asked with a grin.

"No!" she said, but she stopped arguing with him. Sitting down in her chair, she pretended to ignore him as she turned her attention to her computer screen.

"You ready to go home, honey?" Jim asked Carrie, leaning over her chair to give her a kiss.

"Can I have about fifteen minutes? I'll be finished then."

"Sure. Where's Will?"

"He went home to see if he needed to help Viv with the evening." Carrie kept typing as she talked.

"Okay. Come on, David. Will's got some good magazines in here," Jim ordered. The two men went into Will's office and closed the door.

Alex turned and stared at the closed door, irritation on her face.

Carrie smiled at Alex. "Alex, if Jim thought he was in real trouble, he'd be forcing him to make some changes. You can tell by Jim's attitude that David is all right."

"Do you think so?" Alex asked.

"Definitely. You saw how he tore out of here when he wasn't sure David was safe."

"That's true. Thank you, Carrie, for telling me that."

"I just don't want you to worry." She stood. "Now that we've talked, I can leave. Remember, you and David can come to the house whenever you're ready. Will told you that before he left, didn't he? You don't have to wait until six to head over there."

"I know. It might be best if we go early and David can meet each of his sisters one at a time."

"That's a good point, Alex. And Jim and I won't be long at home. We don't live far away."

"Good. David relies on Jim already."

Chapter Six

David rang the doorbell at Will's home, grabbing Alex's hand as he did so.

The door swung open to reveal an older man.

Alex reached out her right hand. "You must be Peter. I'm Alexandra Buford and this is David Buford, Jim's brother."

"Come right in. Mr. Will said you'd be here early. He and Miz Vivian are in the den. Come this way."

"We shouldn't have come early," David whispered as they moved down the wide hall passing several closed doors. They heard some laughter as they drew close to an open door. Just as they reached it, a small boy came running out.

"Hi, Peter!" the child said, hugging Peter's knees. Then he looked at David. "Uncle Jim?" he asked, looking a little confused.

"This must be Danny," Alex said, bending down to greet him on his level.

"Yes, I'm Danny. Who are you?"

"My name is Alex. I work for your daddy."

"Oh." The child leaned closer. "Is that Uncle Jim?"

"No, it's his brother, David."

"Danny? Come back, dear," a soft feminine voice called.

Danny gave them a wide smile. "That's Mommy." He turned and ran back into the room.

The threesome followed. Peter announced, "Ms. Alexandra Buford and Mr. David Buford."

"I wondered who Danny was talking to!" Vivian exclaimed as she came forward, followed by Will. "Welcome, Alex. Will has been raving about how good you are at your job. And, David, I'm so glad you've come to meet your family. They're very anxious to see you."

"Thank you, Mrs. Greenfield," David said. "It's very kind of you to welcome us into your home."

Vivian leaned forward to hug David. "I hope you'll consider this home your home, too. After all, you are Vanessa's brother. And please call me Vivian."

"Thank you, Vivian."

Will shook David's hand and gave Alex a small hug. "Come in and sit down. We're playing with Danny, but I promise he'll head for the kitchen when we eat."

"He doesn't get to eat with us?" Alex asked. "We'd enjoy his company." She took Danny's hand when he came to her side.

"He'll be having his own party with the other little

ones. Joey and Jamie, Rebecca's children, will be there, too."

"Rebecca has two children?" David asked in surprise.

"Yes, and Rachel is expecting her first child in a couple of months."

"They drove up yesterday and are staying with Rebecca and Jeff," Will explained.

"And Vanessa?" David asked.

"She should be here anytime. She's been quite busy, working on her doctorate in psychology." They could all hear the pride in Vivian's voice.

"That's wonderful," Alex said. "It must be a very interesting study."

"Oh, yes, it is," Vivian said. "But we all try to be careful what we say around her. She loves to psychoanalyze us."

"That must be weird," David said.

Will laughed. "Vivian exaggerates. Vanessa is a delightful young woman."

"She was a tiny baby the last time I saw her." David raised his head as he heard a woman's voice in the hallway.

Danny, too, reacted. Leaving Alex's side, he began running toward the door. When a tall, graceful young woman entered, he leaped for her, his arms outstretched. "'Nessa, I missed you!"

She scooped the little boy up and hugged him. "I missed you, too, Danny."

"Darling," Vivian interjected, gesturing at Alex and David, "this is Alex Buford, Will's new employee, and her cousin and your brother, David Buford."

Vanessa let Danny return to the floor and stared at David. Then she imitated Danny, almost leaping into David's embrace.

"Oh, David, I'm so glad we found you!" she said as she stepped back, tears in her eyes. "Now we can all be together."

"Except for Wally," David added.

"Yes. Jim always feels guilty when we mention Wally because he followed Jim into the Marines."

"I know it's not Jim's fault. He's pretty protective of his family. I've already experienced that," David added with a laugh.

"What do you mean?" Vanessa asked.

"I had a little...incident today. Before I knew it, Jim was there."

"Darling," Vivian interjected again, "I know you're excited about David, but you shouldn't ignore Alex."

"Oh!" Vanessa exclaimed, her cheeks turning red. "No, I'm so sorry! Please forgive me, Alex."

"Of course I will. I would've reacted the same way if I was meeting my brother for the first time."

"Thank you. So you and David are cousins?" Vanessa asked.

"Yes. I was five when I first met him."

"How old was he?"

"He was eight, and he definitely thought he was in charge."

Vanessa looked from Alex to David. Then she said, "Ah."

Vivian laughed. "Careful, Vanessa. I warned them you would try to psychoanalyze them."

"Mom, you didn't!"

"I'm afraid I did."

Before anyone could say anything else, Peter escorted Jim and Carrie into the room. Vivian hugged them both, then asked Carrie how she was feeling.

"Fine," Carrie replied. "I'll just be glad when I get to the second trimester so I'm not so tired all the time."

"I understand exactly how you feel," Vivian said.

Vanessa had taken a seat next to Alex. "I'm glad someone else hasn't been pregnant, Alex. I was getting tired of being the only one who hasn't had a baby or isn't in the middle of a pregnancy."

Alex chuckled. "Well, when you do get pregnant, hopefully after a beautiful wedding, you'll know exactly what to expect."

"I hadn't thought of that. I suppose that is a good thing." Vanessa laughed, then asked, "Are you planning a wedding soon, Alex?"

Alex was taken aback. "No, I'm not. Are you?"

"No. It's hard to find men like my brothers. And I don't think I'll be satisfied with anything less."

Alex looked at David and Jim, both tall, sexy men,

and murmured, "I can see the problem. They are really special, aren't they?"

"Yes. Of course, Mom found a good one, so I shouldn't give up hope. And Rebecca and Rachel, too."

"I do like Will. He's a great boss."

"He's not bad as a stepfather, either," Vanessa said with a grin.

Peter now appeared with Rachel and J. D. Stanley, and Rebecca and Jeff Jacobs.

David had more memory of the twins. Alex could see the emotion in his eyes as he met the two young women as adults, along with their husbands. When he glanced around for the children, Rebecca laughed.

"I'm afraid they are much more interested in Betty and Peter. You'll get to meet them after dinner."

"Did you hear that, Danny?" Will said. "Joey and Jamie are in the kitchen with Betty. Do you want to go with Peter so you can play with your cousins? I think Betty has some special treats for you all."

After Peter left, Vivian said, "Betty has some special treats for us, too."

J.D., owner of a ranch in West Texas, said, "I hope so. I was counting on her feeding us well."

Rachel swatted his arm. "You make it sound like you're starving, J.D. Rebecca made us a lovely lunch."

"It was great, but it was six hours ago. Takes a lot of food to keep me going."

Everyone laughed, especially as the door opened and Betty brought in two plates of hors d'oeuvres.

"Here you are, Betty," J.D. greeted her. "I've missed you!"

"I've missed feeding you, Mr. J.D. You look like you've lost weight."

"Well, when Rachel was first pregnant, a lot of things made her sick, so I had to give them up for a while, too. You know how it is."

"That I do. And I'm proud of you putting your wife's comfort in front of your stomach."

Everyone laughed.

Jeff said, "You couldn't tell he was suffering from the amount he had at lunch. I went home to join them and almost didn't get anything to eat."

"Here you go, Mr. Jeff. I made your favorites," Betty said.

"Betty likes to feed hungry men," Vanessa whispered to Alex. "But she eventually remembers us mere females."

Carrie heard Vanessa's remark. "You'll have to admit, we never run out of food, and she does make your favorites, too."

"I know. She takes good care of us. I guess that's why I still live at home," Vanessa admitted. She looked at Alex. "Do you still live at home?"

"No, my mother and David's mother share a house. It would be hard enough to live with my mother, but I don't really get along with David's."

"Why not?" Vanessa asked.

"Mmm, well, she likes to be the center of attention…all the time. She expects David to be at her beck and call constantly. And he tries. But she's never satisfied."

"She doesn't sound like a lot of fun," Vanessa said.

"Don't say that to David. He'll try to defend her," Alex warned, as she glanced across the room and saw David talking to the twins.

"So did he have a happy childhood?" Vanessa asked.

"Yes, I suppose so. His father was there to take care of his mother until a few years ago. David went into the family business and ended up running it. He's done an incredible job, and his mother certainly enjoys her share of the profits."

"Does she have a job?" Vanessa asked.

Alex laughed. "Absolutely not. That's what men are for."

"Oh, dear. I don't think I like her, either."

Alex frowned. "I shouldn't have said so much. I'm probably a little biased. David has accomplished so much, but I'm not sure he gets credit for it."

"I won't say anything," Vanessa promised.

Alex relaxed. She figured Vanessa would keep her word, like David and Jim. It seemed to be a Barlow trait.

David called her over and introduced her to his twin sisters, too. She liked both of them. And, as Carrie had pointed out, all David's sisters were beauties. Alex was surprised, however, when Rebecca pointed out that she looked a lot like them.

"Oh, no, I can't compare with you three," she protested.

"I think she does," David said. "I always thought of the three of you when I was around Alex."

"Well, you certainly didn't show it!" Alex exclaimed. Everyone laughed.

"No, I didn't," David agreed. "I was trying hard not to remember my old family."

"Why, David?" Jim asked.

It took several moments for David to answer. "Mom told me I should never think about my birth family. I was disloyal to her and Dad if I did."

"How terrible!" Vivian exclaimed.

"Yes. I should've ignored her," David said, his head down.

Jim crossed to David's side. "No, Vivian didn't mean you were terrible. She means your mother was terrible to tell you that. I bet you were just a little boy when she began telling you that."

"Of course I wasn't talking about you when I said that was terrible," Vivian said. "I think it was very wrong of your mother to try to get rid of your memories!"

David raised his head. "I appreciate your understanding my situation. I…I need to forgive myself. And be grateful that you found me."

Alex stood aside as the Barlows participated in a

warm group hug. She thought about David's old rigidity about his adopted mother. Maybe now she understood. Even when her mom was upset with her, Alex had never doubted her mother's love. It seemed David didn't have that security.

Betty returned and told them dinner was served.

David moved to Alex's side. "Sorry if I embarrassed you," he murmured.

She took his hand. "Of course you didn't. Aunt June's behavior was awful."

"That's why I didn't want to acknowledge Jim when we first met. I figured he'd hate me for not having done anything about finding him or the others."

"Now you know differently. They all love you," Alex whispered.

David took her hand to go into the dining room. "I haven't done anything to make them love me."

"That's the great thing about family. They love you no matter what."

He squeezed her hand but said nothing else.

THEY STAYED at Will and Vivian's much later than planned. David had felt sure the evening would not last long, but he hadn't counted on finding a loving family just waiting for his appearance.

"They're incredible, aren't they?" he asked as they drove away from the party.

"Yes, they are. You're very lucky."

"I know I am. But you are, too, aren't you? I mean, your mom is nice and you have Janet, Susan and me."

"Yes, of course," she agreed.

"Okay, so you and your mom aren't that close and Janet…well, no one's close to Janet except Mom. But you have Susan and me."

"Yes, and I appreciate that."

A cell phone rang. Alex, driving, frowned and looked around her.

"That's my cell," David said. "I left it in your car while we were inside. Do you mind if I answer it?"

"Of course not." She continued driving while he held the phone to his ear and said little.

When he closed the phone and remained silent, she asked, "David, is something wrong?"

"What time is it?"

"It's almost eleven-thirty. Why? Is your mom expecting you to do something for her?"

"No. That was the Plano Fire Department. My condo burned down tonight."

Alex stared straight ahead as her mind dealt with his words. "Your condo burned down? David, that's dreadful. How…? What are you going to do? Is everything destroyed?"

"I won't know until I get there."

Alex pressed down on the accelerator.

"Don't get a ticket, Alex."

"No, I won't, but…isn't it strange that such a thing should happen to you after you were shot at today?"

"Don't read anything into this, honey. It's just a co-incidence."

"I think I should call Jim."

"No!"

"Why not? Afraid of what he'll say?" she asked, a challenge in her voice.

"No, I'd like him to think of me as a man, not a cowardly little boy!"

"Jim wouldn't. He just wants to keep you safe."

"I'm planning on being safe!" He sat silent for a minute. "Honey, I'm not taking any chances. If the fire was arson, I'll start putting in the security Jim recommended."

"You promise?"

"Yes."

Alex took a deep breath. "Okay."

The fire trucks were still on the scene when they reached David's condo. Fortunately, the condos had a firewall between each, so none of the units burned except David's. They got out of the car and approached a policeman standing nearby. David introduced himself and asked if he could look more closely at his belongings.

"I doubt you can. There's nothing left. We're looking for the cause of the fire now."

David just stood there staring at what had once been his home.

Alex slid her hand into his.

"Let's go!" he said. "There's nothing here."

"You should give the policeman your office number before we go."

"Oh, yeah." He turned back to the policeman and gave him his business card. "Please let me know the outcome as soon as possible."

"Certainly, Mr. Buford."

David took Alex's hand. "Okay, we can go now."

"Where do you want to go?" Alex asked.

"It's almost midnight. I hate to do it, but I guess I'd better call Pete. He's got a couch he'll let me sleep on."

"Wait!" Alex said, reaching out to put a hand on his cell phone. "That's ridiculous. I have a second bedroom. You can stay there tonight."

"Alex, I'm not sure that's a good idea. I mean, people might not realize I'm your cousin. It might start talk."

"David, this isn't the nineteen-fifties. I'll be just fine. If anyone says anything, I'll tell them to mind their own business."

"You're sure you don't mind?"

"Positive."

She started the car and headed for her own condo, not too far away. It was a relief to see her home safe and undisturbed. With a sigh of relief, she pulled into the garage beneath her condo. "I'm sorry it's too late to get you any clothes tonight, but we can go shopping early tomorrow morning for a few items, at least."

"I don't want to make you late for your job."

"Will won't mind when he hears what has happened."

"Why would you tell Will? It's not any of his business."

"Maybe because you'll be hiring Jim to set up security at your company? And maybe taking his advice on a safe place to live?"

"I think I can find a place to live by myself, Alex."

She whirled around to stare at him. "Don't you realize you'd be dead already if you'd been home tonight? That might not matter to you, but it matters to a few of us!"

"You're right, honey. That was dumb of me to say that. And I'm glad I was out this evening. Something else I owe my family."

"Come on," she said, and led the way to her condo.

Chapter Seven

Alex walked into her condo and quickly picked up a couple of things that were out of place. "Sorry, I wasn't prepared for company."

"I'm not company, Alex. It's certainly going to be more comfortable than Pete's couch," David said.

"I hope so. I forgot to ask. Do you have fire insurance?"

"Yes. I'll call my agent in the morning. There shouldn't be any problem."

"Oh, good, then you'll be able to replace at least most of your stuff," Alex said.

"You sound like you think that should be fun," David said. "I think it will be awful."

"Shopping, when you have the money, is a lot of fun, David. But if you don't like it, I'll be glad to help you."

"Be careful what you offer. I may take you up on that. A lot of my furnishings came from my college days. I'll need some help picking out some nice furniture."

Alex was taking clean sheets out of her hall closet

and she turned to stare at David. "Are you serious? Susan and I could do the job. We'd have so much fun!"

"I'm not sure about Susan. Her tastes are a little...unusual."

"No, she'd be great. Haven't you been in her condo?"

"No."

Alex stared at him. "You haven't? But she moved to her condo a year ago."

"I've been busy," he said defensively.

"You haven't visited your baby sister's condo for a year?"

"Okay, Alex, I've been neglectful, but can we get past that tonight so I can get some sleep? I'm tired."

"I guess so," she muttered. Then she turned and led him to her second bedroom. She pulled the spread off the bed and began putting sheets on it. David helped.

"Here's a blanket," Alex said, pulling one from the closet. "That and the spread should keep you warm enough."

"I'll be fine, Alex. Thanks."

"Great," she muttered.

David caught her arm as she tried to leave the room. "You're mad at me and I don't know why."

She whirled around. "How can you do that to Susan? You're the only man in her life and you haven't even visited her home? How do you think that makes her feel?"

"I don't know. It never occurred to me."

"Well, I'm not sure you deserve your new family

when you aren't taking care of your old family!" Alex stomped out of the extra bedroom, leaving David standing alone.

After a minute he came out of the bedroom, looking for her. "Alex?"

She stepped out of the kitchen, a glass of water in her hand. "Yes?"

"I apologize and I'll visit Susan's condo as soon as possible."

"Fine!"

"I'm going to go to bed now, if that's all right."

"Yes, of course. There's a bathroom connected to your bedroom."

"Thank you, Alex," David said, and leaned forward to kiss her on the cheek. Then he disappeared into his bedroom.

Alex stood there for several minutes. She regretted being angry with David. After all, he'd been through a lot today. He'd been shot at, met his family and lost his home.

She finished her glass of water and decided to go to bed, too. Tomorrow was another day, and she was sure David would keep his word about installing security at his office.

WHEN THE ALARM WOKE ALEX the next morning, she sniffed the air. Mmm. Coffee and frying bacon. She grabbed her robe and hurried to the kitchen.

There was David, standing over the stove. "Good

morning. I thought I should cook breakfast since you let me stay here. Sit down. I'll bring you a cup of coffee."

"Thank you. I didn't expect such service."

"I appreciate you taking me in last night. Oh, and I remembered last night that I had a lot of clothes at the cleaners. So I *have* some clothes. I called the place when it opened at seven, and my cleaning is ready to be picked up."

He was dressed in the clothes he'd worn last night.

"We can go there as soon as I get dressed."

"Okay. I'll call Pete after breakfast to let him know I'll be late this morning," David said as he brought her a cup of coffee.

Alex jumped up and went to the front door and opened it to find her morning paper there, waiting for her. She brought it back to the kitchen, and sat down, scanning it for mention of the fire last night.

"Here it is," Alex said as David put a plate with eggs and bacon on the table. Then he put a plate of toast down before he joined her to look at the article.

"Does it give a cause for the fire?" he asked. Alex handed him that portion of the paper. "Suspicious circumstances," he read out loud.

"Time to call Jim," Alex said.

"I'll wait until I get to the office and see if the fire department has called. This 'suspicious circumstances' isn't exactly proof of arson."

Alex took a bite of the breakfast David had prepared, saying nothing.

After a moment David said, "I'll keep my word, Alex. I just want to be sure."

"Okay."

When her plate was empty, she rose to her feet. "I'll clean up the kitchen as soon as I get dressed. You can just leave everything and go call Pete."

She didn't wait to see what he would do. After a quick shower, she dressed and blew her hair dry. Then she put on a little face powder and some lipstick and was ready to go.

David was cleaning the kitchen when she came out. "I told you I'd clean the kitchen, David. You didn't have to do that. After all, you cooked."

"I was ready and you weren't. But I'll admit I didn't think you'd be ready in such a short time."

"I'm ready. Let's go to the cleaners."

"Okay." He put the last of the dishes in the dishwasher and followed her down the stairs to the garage. "I like your having a garage. That's a real safety factor."

"Yes, it is. Maybe you should look for something like this when you look for a new place."

"Good idea."

After they picked up his cleaning, Alex suggested they go to Target so he could buy some essentials that he no longer had. He agreed. When their shopping was done, he suddenly declared, "I don't know where to take everything."

"My place," she replied without hesitation.

David said nothing as she drove back to her condo and began to help him take everything to his room.

"Alex," he finally protested, "I really shouldn't stay here again. I can get a hotel room until I find a place."

"There's no need for that, David. I have room. You can stay here until you have a new place. It's no big deal."

He said nothing else. After they got everything in his room, he closed the door behind Alex and changed into clean clothes. When he emerged in a suit and yesterday's tie, Alex thought, not for the first time, how handsome he was.

She immediately suggested they leave for his office. Such thoughts would get her in trouble.

"Did you call Pete?"

"Yeah. He'll be on top of things."

When they reached his building, Alex pulled up in front of the door. "Will your car be ready today?"

"No, I think they'll need another day."

"Then I'll pick you up. Stay at work, inside your office, until I call and tell you I'm waiting."

"Honey, you make it sound downright dangerous," David said with a little laugh.

Alex ignored his attempt to make light of his situation. "You call me as soon as you find out how the fire started, okay?"

"Yeah, I'll call you. Now quit worrying and get to your job."

When Alex arrived, she first apologized for being

late. Then she told Jim about the fire. "David's not taking it seriously, but it seems too coincidental to me."

"What did the fire department say about the cause of the fire?" Jim asked.

"The newspaper said the fire was under investigation or something like that. David said he'd call me once he'd heard from the fire department. Has he called?"

Carrie shook her head. "Not that I know of." She got up from her chair and walked to Will's door. "Will, did David call before we got here?"

"No. Should he have?"

"His condo burned last night."

Will came out of his office. "How terrible! Before or after he got home?"

"Before," Alex said. "He's supposed to call me here and let me know the cause of the fire as soon as he finds out. If it was arson, he promised to put into place all the security measures Jim recommended."

"Good job, Alex," Jim said. "Why don't you call him now?"

She picked up the phone and dialed David's number from memory. "David, we're all anxious. Did you hear from the fire department?"

She listened, said little, and when she hung up the phone, Jim stepped forward. "Well?"

"Yes, the fire was set deliberately, but David has been dealing with *another* problem. Someone broke into the company building. When they couldn't find what they were looking for, they did as much damage as possible." She paused, then said, "He wanted to know if you could come out and help him take some immediate steps to improve security."

"Let me check with Will."

"I forgot to say he's willing to pay for your help," Alex called out.

Carrie smiled at her. "That wouldn't matter. Where's David staying?"

"With me. I have two bedrooms."

"Oh, I see," Carrie said.

"David was going to sleep on Pete Dansky's couch. But that seemed silly to me when I have an unused bedroom."

"You're right. After all, he's your cousin. That was generous of you. Will he look for another condo right away?"

"I suppose, but I want him to find a safer place. Someone is after him."

"It would seem that way. Otherwise, it would be just too coincidental to be shot at and have his home burn down on the same day."

"And his company broken into," Alex added.

"That's right. What a lot to happen to you in twenty-four hours!"

Jim came out of Will's office. "I'm heading over to David's office. I'll call you, Carrie, and let you know when I'll be back."

"Be careful," Carrie said, after receiving his kiss.

"I will, honey. Don't worry."

"No, of course not," Carrie said with a smile that remained on her face until Jim left the office. Then she laid her head on her desk.

"Carrie, are you all right?"

She raised her head and smiled at Alex. "Sorry, it's those hormones. I don't want Jim to know I worry, but I do."

"I know. I'm worried about David, too, but I have to hide it. Keeping busy helps."

"True. But, Alex, I just want to say I'm glad you're here. I go crazy when I'm by myself."

Alex gave her a shaky smile. "I'm glad I'm helping someone."

DAVID HAD CALLED his insurance agent as soon as he got to the office, explaining about the break-in at the office, as well as the loss of his condo and contents to fire. The man promised to talk to the fire department, as well as the police.

Pete walked into his office. "You should've called me last night. My couch isn't too uncomfortable."

"I appreciate it, Pete, but Alex has a spare bedroom and bath. I stayed there last night."

"Is that wise?" Pete asked hesitantly.

David's head snapped up. "She's my cousin."

"But you were adopted, so she's not really kin to you."

"We used separate bedrooms, Pete."

"Okay, I won't say anything else. But have you talked to the fire department? Was the fire accidental?"

"Apparently not. They suspect arson."

"Man, I'm getting worried. Seems like someone is out to get you."

"Yeah, I know. I promised Alex I'd call Jim and put in some of his security ideas."

"I'm all for that."

"It won't be just me. *You're* going to need to be observant, too. I mean, you're as important to the company as I am."

"No, I'm not, David."

"I rely on you. You're second in command."

"Then I'd better make sure my fire insurance is current, because I don't have a cousin I could move in with," Pete said with a grin.

When Alex called a few minutes later, David kept his promise and asked that Jim come help him install some security measures.

After that, David called Pete. "I want to know where we are in our bid. Did the break-in compromise our target date?"

"No," Pete said. "We should be finished by the end of the day today."

"Terrific. That should take some of the pressure off."

"I hope so. Have you got a minute, David? I want to talk to you about a new project."

"Sure, come to my office. I'll want you here when Jim arrives, anyway."

Soon the two of them were looking over some papers at David's desk. When they heard a scream, they jumped to their feet to head for the reception area where Jeannie was seated.

But before they even reached the door, it slammed back against the wall and two masked men entered, guns at the ready.

David raised his hands and began moving back toward his desk. Pete followed suit.

"Which one of you is Buford?" one of the men asked in a growl.

"You've got the wrong office. He's down the hall," David said.

"Okay, I'll shoot both of you just to be sure."

"I'm Buford," David said quickly. "Leave him out of it." He looked at Pete. "Go back to your office," David ordered.

"Call the police!" Pete yelled, not knowing if Jeannie was still out there in the reception area.

Both men took aim at them, and David and Pete dropped and rolled to avoid the bullets.

But David felt a searing pain in his right shoulder and knew he'd been hit, though he wasn't sure how bad the wound was. He heard more bullets and looked up in time to see Jim with his gun drawn. He saw Pete lying still on the other side of the room. The only thing he could do was scoot to his phone and call the police.

Suddenly the two men knocked Jim down and ran out the door. Jim immediately got up and gave chase, despite David's call for him to come back.

David rose to his feet and, gripping his wounded shoulder, staggered across the floor to Pete's side. "Pete? Are you all right?"

Pete slowly opened his eyes. "I...I don't know," he gasped.

"Just lie still. I'm going to see if anyone's called an ambulance."

David dragged himself to the outer office. "Jeannie?"

Shaking, she got up from behind her desk. "Are you all right?" she asked.

"Not really. Call an ambulance and the police. And tell them to hurry. Pete's in bad shape."

"Yes, sir!"

Susan appeared in the hallway. "What happened?"

"Some men broke in with guns," David said.

"David, you're hurt!" He looked down and saw the blood seeping through the fingers over his wound.

"Pete's worse," he muttered.

Susan made a mad dash to Pete's side.

David felt his legs crumple as he sank to the floor.

Suddenly strong arms were around him. "Hang in there, David," Jim said. "The ambulance is on its way."

"I'm more worried about Pete."

"You're both going to be all right. Wait here and I'll check on Pete."

David lay on the floor, anxious for word on Pete.

Jim found a young woman holding Pete in her arms.

"Excuse me, ma'am. May I look at his injury?"

"Are you a doctor?" she asked in a sob.

"No, but I've had some experience with wounds. He's bleeding a lot, isn't he?"

"Yes, he's hit in the head."

"Pete?" Jim called.

Again Pete managed to open his eyes. "Yeah? Jim, is that you?"

"Yup. You've got a head wound, Pete, but I don't think it's serious. It just bleeding a lot. The ambulance is on its way. This young lady will stay with you until help arrives."

He went back to David. "Hey, brother? I'm counting on you pulling through."

David, who'd been on the verge of losing consciousness, pulled himself together. "Yeah. How's Pete?"

"He's actually in better shape than you. He has a head injury, but it's not serious." Jim paused before he said, "He's luckier in another way, too. He's got some young lady holding him and crying over him."

"Susan," David managed to say.

"Susan? Does she work here?"

"Yeah, but…but she's also my little sister."

"Sir, if you'll move out of our way?" an unknown voice said.

"Yes, I will," Jim replied. "There's another injured man in there." He pointed to the office door.

The two paramedics split up.

Jim followed the man into the office, knowing someone would have to handle Susan.

"Susan, let the man take care of Pete," he said, pulling her away to give the man room.

"I have to stay with Pete. He needs me!"

"I'm sure he does, but he needs to stop losing blood most of all. I'll take you to the hospital right behind the ambulance."

"What if he dies on the way? I should go with him."

"David has to go in the ambulance, Susan. There won't be room for you."

"David? Oh, I forgot he got hurt, too!"

Chapter Eight

When the two injured men were loaded into the ambulance, with an assurance from one of the paramedics, Jim led Susan to his car. "Come on, I'll take you to the hospital."

"But I don't know who you are!" she exclaimed.

"I'm Jim Barlow, David's brother."

Susan's head snapped up. "David is *my* brother! What do you mean?"

"David was adopted when our parents were killed in a car accident. We recently found each other."

She looked confused. Jim took out his cell phone. "Honey, is Alex there?"

"Yes, Jim. Is everything all right?"

"There's been a bit of trouble. David and Pete are on their way to the hospital. I need Alex to tell Susan it's okay to go with me. And Alex might want to come to the hospital, too."

Suddenly Alex was on the line. "Alex, there's been

a little problem. Do you want to meet us at the hospital out here? And please tell Susan it's safe to go with me."

Of course, it wasn't that simple. He had to reassure Alex that David was all right, and then Alex had to convince Susan to go with him. When he finally had Susan in the car, he sped to the hospital.

In the E.R., fortunately, it was a slow time and doctors were available to look at the two men at once. Jim provided the necessary identification and other details. He suggested the two be put in the same room.

Pete's wound, in spite of all the blood, was superficial. The bullet had just grazed the edge of his head. They expected to keep him overnight and then release him the next morning.

David's wound was a little more serious. The bullet in his right shoulder had torn through tendons, just missing an artery.

Pete had already been taken to a room, accompanied by Susan, when Alex arrived. Though she was concerned, she was in control of her emotions. Jim comforted her and told her about David's wound.

"What happened to the two shooters?"

"I got to David's office as they fired the first bullets. I pulled my gun and wounded at least one of them. I followed them out of the building, after I checked to be sure David and Pete were alive and told the secretary to call 911. Then I got the license-plate number and gave it to the police when they arrived."

"So they'll be able to find them?"

"They should be. Now that you're here for David, I'm going to go to the competing company, Carey & Company. It's hard to believe that they would be behind this attack, but I want to find out."

"Just be careful. I promised Carrie I would tell you that." She gave him a hug and then waved goodbye as he left the E.R.

Then she walked to the desk and asked if she could see David. When they asked if she was family, she said yes, his cousin.

When she saw him being bandaged, she had to fight her rush of emotion. It was important that she didn't fall apart.

She moved to his other side and touched his face. He opened his eyes and gave her a weak smile. "Hi. How are you doing?" he asked.

"I'm the one who should be asking you that question," she said. "How could this happen?"

"Someone doesn't like me."

She leaned down and kissed his forehead. "Well, you're safe now. Pete's already gone to the room you two are going to share."

"Ma'am, we have a private room for each of them," one of the nurses said.

"No, we need to keep them together. They'll be easier to protect that way," Alex explained.

"Surely you don't expect someone to come after them here?"

"It's definitely a possibility."

The nurse visibly shuddered. "Yes, we'll put them together. He's ready to go now if you want to walk alongside him."

"Yes, I'd like that. Thanks." Alex moved back beside David and took his left hand in hers. "Ready to go for a ride?"

"Where are we going?" David asked.

She realized he was under the effect of a painkiller and unaware of much. "We're going to see Pete. And probably Susan. Jim said she was beside him when they moved him to a room."

"Why is Susan there?"

"She thinks she loves him, remember?"

"Oh, yeah."

They entered the elevator and moved to the fourth floor. Then they pushed him into a room where Pete and Susan were. Susan was sitting quietly, holding Pete's hand. She seemed startled when she saw Alex.

"Alex! I didn't know you were coming."

"Yeah, Suse, I wanted to be sure David was all right."

Susan didn't leave her seat beside Pete. "How's David doing?"

"Good. He's a little out of it from pain medicine, but he'll be fine."

"Alex, that man, Jim, said he was David's brother. Is that true?"

"Yes. I work with him. That's how he found David."

"But…but David is *my* brother. Is he going to take him away?"

"No, Susan, of course not. But there were six children in his family. David was the last to be found."

"There are six of them?"

"No. One of them died in the Middle East. There are five of them now."

"Alex," David whispered.

"Yes, David?" she asked, turning her attention to him at once.

"Is Pete…?"

"Pete's going to be fine, David. He's sleeping right now, but his wound wasn't serious. He'll be out of here before you."

"I…I…." He finished with a groan.

"David, are you in pain?"

"Yes…."

Alex leaned over him and pressed the button for the nurse, and within minutes, David was given more pain medication. He fell asleep, which Alex guessed was the best thing for him. But she had one problem. She didn't know whether to tell his mother or not. She'd intended to ask him what she should do about that, but now it was too late.

"Susan?" she called softly.

"What?"

"Do you think I should call your mother?"

"Oh—no!"

Alex stepped around the curtain drawn between the two patients. "Why not?"

"She might find out about David's other family. She'd be furious!"

"But, Susan, won't she get worried if she can't find David? Doesn't she usually call him often?"

"Yes, but she calls him on his cell phone most of the time. Can't he just keep it by his bed and answer it?"

"I don't think so. Maybe she won't call today and he can decide what to do about her tomorrow."

"That sounds like a good idea, Alex. I don't think she'd bother to visit him even if she knew."

Alex agreed, but it made her sad that her family had so little of the warmth the Barlows had.

"Susan, do you want to go home? You can take my car if you do."

Susan looked alarmed. "No, I can't go home and leave Pete alone. He doesn't have any family to stay with him. I think it's important to have someone with you if you're in the hospital."

"But I'll be here with both Pete and David. I'll make sure he's all right."

"Why should you get to stay and not me?"

"Because I'm here to protect them."

"Protect them? From what?" Susan asked, her voice rising.

"Shh! Susan, I was a cop. Now I'm a private investigator. I carry a gun."

"So? No one would…I mean, surely they wouldn't… No! I don't believe it! Why would anyone…?"

"I don't know, Suse, but we have to be sure they're safe. That's why Jim had them put in the same room." She watched comprehension wash over Susan's face.

"You mean those men *meant* to shoot Pete and David?"

Alex drew a deep breath. "Well, Susan, they sure didn't pick that building at random and go specifically to the president's office to find someone to shoot. It doesn't happen that way."

"How are you going to protect them?"

"Shh, Susan. I told you I carry a gun."

"Well…you'll need help. I can help."

"Honey, you should just go home until tomorrow. We should have things cleared up by then." She hoped Susan couldn't see that she was lying. She didn't want her cousin in any danger unless it was necessary.

"No! I won't go. I'm staying with Pete."

Alex sighed. "Okay, let's wait until we hear from Jim."

AFTER LEAVING THE HOSPITAL, Jim contacted the police. The police told him they had checked the license plate on the gunmen's car. They'd located the two men and had already arrested them. But the men refused to say who had hired them.

Jim reached the police station and asked to talk to the officer in charge of the investigation. He explained why he was there, both as an investigator and a brother of one of the victims. Then he suggested they try to con the shooters by telling them they already knew who hired them, naming the owner of Carey & Company.

"Why do you suspect the owner of that particular company?" the officer asked.

Jim explained about the young woman who had spied on David's company. He also suggested they check with the fire department and see if they could pin arson on these guys, too.

Jim watched through the two-way mirror as two detectives went in to interview them. They got a confession from them within ten minutes. They left the building to arrest the owner of Carey & Company. Jim left for the hospital.

When he reached the room, it was close to six o'-clock. He'd talked to Carrie to tell her he hoped to be home soon. When he opened the door, Alex jumped up from her chair, ready to face an adversary if necessary.

"It's just me, Alex."

"Oh, Jim, I'm glad to see you. Did you make any progress?"

He grinned. "Yeah, lots. It was the owner of Carey & Co. The police have gone to bring him in. Those guys said the man was unstable, that his company was about to go under if they didn't get this bid David's been working on."

"That's crazy!" Alex exclaimed softly.

Susan appeared at the end of the curtain. "What's going on?"

"Were we too loud?" Alex asked. Then she said, "Jim says they've found the man who hired the men to shoot David and Pete. He was the one who sent the woman to spy on them and report their work, the one you replaced. He was afraid his company would go bankrupt if he didn't win the bid."

"That's awful."

"Yes, but it means we don't have to protect the guys all night."

"Are you sure?" Susan asked, looking back over her shoulder.

"Well, I don't think it will be necessary," Jim said.

"I think I'll stay until after David eats his dinner. Would you like to stay with me, Susan? We can go home after the guys are ready to go to sleep."

"Oh, yes, I'd like that."

"Okay, I'm going on home, then," Jim said. "Carrie is waiting for me."

"I bet she is. Thanks for helping us out, Jim," Alex said, hugging his neck.

Susan gave him a hug, too.

"Alex, call if anything worries you," Jim said from

the doorway as he was leaving. "Will you be in to work in the morning?"

"Yes, I may be a little late. I want to come by the hospital and check on David and Pete first."

"Good. Tell David I'll be here at lunchtime to check on him."

"He'll like that, Jim. Good night, and thanks again."

After the door closed behind Jim, Alex turned to smile at Susan. "What a relief."

"Yes. But this is all so hard to believe. At least we don't have to worry about another attack on them."

"Let me give you some money and you can go to the cafeteria and get some hamburgers for us. They'll be bringing the guys' food soon and one of us should be here."

Luckily, Susan didn't question why she should go instead of Alex. Alex couldn't give a real reason, but she wanted to make sure that no one came in to hurt the two men—just in case everyone hadn't gotten the word that the plot was over.

When Susan got back with the food, they shoved the curtain aside that divided the two men and sat between their beds, whispering about the events of the day as they ate.

Pete awoke first. When the first word out of his mouth was Susan, she popped up out of her chair, her hamburger in her hand, to answer him. She explained that he and David were out of danger.

"And David? Is he okay?"

Alex answered him. "He's fine. He's still asleep over here beside you."

Pete pushed up on his elbows to see for himself. "Are you sure he's okay?"

Alex took David's hand and squeezed it. "David? Can you wake up? Pete wants to know you're all right."

It took a minute, but David finally opened his eyes. Alex kissed his cheek. "Good job, David. Pete was worried about you."

"Where's Pete?" he immediately asked.

"Over here," Susan said. "How are you, David? I'm glad you're all right."

"Thanks, Susan. What are you doing here?"

"I…I…."

Alex leaned over to whisper, "She came for Pete."

"Oh."

"David," Susan began, "Jim said he was your brother."

"Yeah, is he here?" David asked, glancing around the room.

"No, but he was," Alex said. "He managed to help the police solve the crime. Apparently, the owner of Carey & Company went off the deep end because he was going bankrupt—unless he got the bid you were both going for."

"Damn," David said.

"Yes, and Jim said since you were safe, he'd go on home, because Carrie was waiting for him. But he said he'd see you tomorrow at lunch."

"Good," David said, relaxing against his pillow.

"Your dinner should be coming soon. Are you hungry?" Alex asked.

"Not very. I'm not sure I can manage to eat."

"I'm going to feed you, David. That's what I stayed for," she assured him with a smile.

Pete said, "I'm hungry. Are you going to feed me, Susan?"

"If you don't mind," Susan said.

Alex wanted to tell Pete he'd have another hit in the head if he disappointed Susan. She'd suffered all day long.

Fortunately, Pete was in no danger. "I'd love that."

With perfect timing, the door opened and a woman brought in a tray to Pete. Then she returned with a tray for David.

"Are you going to feed 'em?" the woman asked.

"Yes, we will," Alex said.

She uncovered the plate and found a large serving of meat loaf, some mashed potatoes and carrots. "I think they cooked your favorites, David," she teased.

"What is it?"

"Meat loaf."

"Woulda been better if it was a steak."

"You should stick with the meat loaf until you're well."

"When do I get to go home?" David demanded.

"Yeah," Pete agreed. "I feel well enough to go home tonight."

"Neither of you is going home tonight. Pete might

get out tomorrow sometime. I'm not sure about you, David, but you'll stay until they say you're ready, and not a minute before!" Alex insisted.

"Who died and made you king?" David demanded.

"Jim left me in charge. You can argue with him."

"Aw, that's not fair," David protested.

"Take a bite," Alex ordered.

Susan began feeding Pete, so conversation faded.

Alex noticed David tiring as they'd finished about half of his meal. "David, have you had enough to eat?"

"Yeah. Would you ring for the nurse?"

"What is it? Can't I help you?"

"No, you can't. I need to go to the bathroom!"

"But I could help you to the door and—"

"No! I need to preserve my dignity!"

Without another word, Alex leaned forward and rang for the nurse.

When the nurse reached the room, she asked David what he needed.

David's cheeks turned red. "Don't you have any male nurses?"

The nurse rolled her eyes. "Not tonight. It's me or no one."

"I need to go to the bathroom. Is it okay if I go by myself?"

"I'd better help you the first time out of the bed. You can go in by yourself. I'll just make sure you're keeping your balance."

"Okay, thank you." He pushed back the cover as Alex pushed away the bed table that held his food. Then he swung his feet to the floor. The nurse moved to his side and he started walking to the bathroom.

"You better use your good hand to hold your gown closed in the back," the nurse mentioned casually, and David almost lost his balance to take care of that little problem.

Once he was inside the bathroom, the nurse said, "He's a modest fellow, isn't he?"

"Yes, he is," Alex agreed.

"Most guys don't worry much about their wives seeing—"

"She's not my wife!" David exclaimed as he opened the door.

"Sorry, I just assumed. I mean, both these women seem so dedicated, staying with you ever since you came in, I just assumed... She's not your wife, either?" she asked Pete.

"No, ma'am, I'm not that lucky."

"Well, as soon as I get him in bed," the nurse said, "you want a turn?"

"Yes, please."

Once Pete was also back in bed, Alex made sure David got his pain medicine, checked to see if water was close by for both men, and finally said good-night. David looked so desolate she moved to the head of his bed and kissed his cheek. "I'll be here in the morning about the time you wake up. Go right to sleep so you can wake up early."

She turned to go, but David grabbed her hand. "I don't think I said thanks."

Her smile warmed. "Not necessary. I'll see you in the morning."

Susan told Pete goodbye, and both women walked out together.

"Oh! I forgot," said Susan. "I don't have my car here."

"I'll take you back to the company office so you can get your car. But I thought I'd make a run to the store before it closes and pick up some pajamas for David to preserve his modesty."

"What a good idea. I'll get Pete some, too. Um, is that acceptable?"

"I think so. And maybe we can find something to entertain them with tomorrow."

Chapter Nine

Alex stayed up late to wash and dry the things she'd bought for David. She'd offered to take care of Pete's things, too, but Susan immediately said she'd wash his.

"All right. I'll see you in the morning."

Now, at six-fifteen the next morning, she wished she hadn't promised to be there so early. The stressful events of yesterday had taken a lot out of her.

Finally Alex pushed off the covers and headed for the shower. Then she dressed for work and grabbed a quick breakfast. After gathering up David's new pajamas, she drove to the hospital.

The halls of the hospital were quiet, which made her nervous. She hurried to the room assigned to the two men and rapped on the door. She thought she heard someone say come in, and she opened the door. David was still sleeping, but Pete waved to her.

"Hi, Pete. How are you this morning?" she called

softly. She reached his bedside and took his hand. "Did you have a good night?"

"I must have, because I don't remember anything." His grin made her feel good.

"How about David? How did he do?"

"Okay, as far as I know."

"Good. Any sign of breakfast trays?"

"The nurse told me seven-thirty."

Just as Alex was about to speak, Susan came into the room.

She came to an immediate stop, staring at Pete and Alex. "Am I interrupting something?" she demanded.

Pete turned bright red, but Alex just grinned at her cousin. "Don't be silly, Suse. Pete and I were just talking. After all, David is still asleep and we've got a few minutes before the breakfast trays arrive."

"Well, I wanted to…to give these things to Pete."

Sometimes, it seemed to Alex that Susan was much younger than she was. Then she remembered that Susan had had to deal with her mother, June, and the "princess," her sister, Janet. No wonder she wasn't as sure of herself as she should've been.

"Let me get out of your way, because I bet Pete is eager to see what you've brought him."

Pete was staring at Susan. "You bought me something?"

"Yes, I thought… I know you may go home today,

but I got you something you might need." She handed him the sack.

"Pajamas?" Pete said in surprise. "I've never…I mean, these are nice."

"It's so you don't have to hold your gown together in the back when you get out of bed," Alex explained with a smile.

"What's going on?" David asked crossly from behind Alex.

She whirled around. "You're awake!"

"Of course I am. You were making a lot of noise."

"I thought you'd already be awake when I got here," Alex said, raising her eyebrows.

"I guess I am now."

"No sulking, David," Alex said. "Pete's been perfectly charming."

Susan frowned at her brother. "Really, David! It's not Pete's fault."

"You mean he can't help being charming?" David said.

Pete grinned at his best friend. "That's right, pal. I'm charming!"

"Yeah, right!" David shot back, but he was grinning.

"I brought you something I thought you might need," Alex said, handing David a sack.

He didn't say anything, but he opened the sack. "What is this?" he asked.

"Pajamas, so you could get out of bed without—" she cleared her throat "—exposing yourself."

"Thanks."

Though his thanks hadn't held much enthusiasm, Alex smiled and said, "You're welcome."

David glowered at her. Then he pushed back his covers. "I'll change in the bathroom."

"I'm not sure you can by yourself," Alex said.

His head snapped up. "Are you volunteering?"

"No, I was going to suggest you ask for help from the only other male with two good arms in the room."

"Oh. Uh, Pete, could you help me?"

"Yeah, I think I'd better before you put your foot in your mouth again," Pete said with his friendly grin.

"I didn't do that!" David protested.

Pete closed the door behind them, so the women didn't hear his response to his friend.

"David's a bit of a bear this morning," Susan said.

"I think he didn't have a great night, Susan. He probably needs more painkiller."

"Yeah, I guess. It's just that Pete's so easygoing," Susan said with a dreamy smile.

The bathroom door opened and both men came out with the pajamas on, although David couldn't easily put on the top because of his wound, so he wore his gown over his bottoms.

"Just in time for breakfast," Alex said, having heard the rattle of breakfast trays in the hall.

As Alex helped David to eat his breakfast, she thought he relaxed somewhat. "Have you decided what your employees should be told? I thought about it last night, but it should've occurred to me yesterday afternoon."

"Damn, I should've thought of that!" David said, tensing.

"Relax, David. You were too out of it to do anything about it yesterday. Everyone will understand."

"I can't believe I didn't think… I bet they didn't finish the bid. Pete…."

"It's okay, David. After they release me, I'm sure we can get it finished today."

"You think you'll get out today?" David asked.

Alex heard the longing in his voice. "They said you'd probably get out tomorrow, David, which is pretty good when you consider what you went through."

"But—"

The nurse came into the room. "Have you finished your breakfasts?"

"No, not yet, but we'll hurry," Alex promised. Then she immediately fed David more eggs.

"I don't really want any more," he said.

"If you want out tomorrow, you need to eat what they feed you. It will help you get stronger."

He scowled, but accepted what she fed him.

They had just finished breakfast when the nurse returned.

"The doctor will be in to see both of you in just a minute. Let me take those trays out of the way."

Alex stood. "I guess I'd better go. Oh, David, do you want me to tell your mother?"

"No. I'll be out before she could do anything."

"All right. Jim will be here for lunch. And be sure you eat all your lunch," she added sternly.

"Yes, Mom. When will you be back?"

"I'll come back after work."

"Susan, you'd better get to the office, too," David said.

"But I want to stay here to be with…both of you. You may need help."

"That's what they pay the nurses for. We need you at the office to make sure everyone knows we're all right and to finish up the work on the bid. See Harry when you get there. Tell him he's in charge until Pete gets there."

Alex leaned over and kissed David's cheek. "If you don't speak more kindly to your sister, she may disown you as a brother."

"Susan knows it's just because we need her at work."

Susan frowned at him. "I may know it, but it doesn't mean I like it. Bye, Pete."

She walked out of the room with Alex.

DAVID'S SHOULDER HURT, but he was determined not to ask for pain medicine. When the doctor arrived, he went to Pete first. He checked his wound before looking at the notes the nurse had made.

"Do I get out today, Doc?" Pete asked.

"I'm afraid not, Mr. Dansky. You're running a fever, and until it's gone or we know the cause of it, we're going to have to keep you here a little longer."

"Oh."

"Don't sound so disappointed. It shouldn't be more than another day." He turned to David. "And you have your friend to keep you company. How are you feeling, Mr. Buford?"

"Fine. In fact, I might feel good enough to leave."

"No, you don't. I suspect you're in pain. Why haven't you asked for medicine?"

"Because it makes me fuzzy-headed. I don't like feeling that way."

"But it relaxes your muscles so your wound can heal better. How about I cut the amount by half? That will give you some relief without as much drugging."

"Okay."

When the doctor left the room, David asked his friend, "Do you think I can trust him to cut the dose?"

"What are your choices, David? You have to get well as fast as you can."

David sighed. "I guess so. Are you feeling all right?"

"I do feel a little warm." Pete chuckled. "I thought it was just seeing Susan. But if that was true, you should be feeling warm, too. After all, Alex was here for you."

"She's my cousin," David muttered.

"Yeah, I wondered about that when we went out for steaks. But I didn't know then that you were adopted."

The nurse entered to give them the medicine the doctor had prescribed. A few minutes later they were both asleep.

When Jim reached the hospital room, the staff had just awakened the patients and served lunch. "Anyone in here looking for company?" he asked as he entered.

"Jim! It's good to see you," David said. "I think we owe you a lot."

"Just doing my job, brother," Jim said with a smile.

Pete held out his hand. "I'd like to thank you, Jim. I got the same service and I'm not your brother."

Jim shook his hand. "Hey, we're just lucky those goons weren't such good shots. Once they arrested them, it wasn't too hard to have them cave and give the name of the man who hired them."

"But how did they find those guys so quickly?" David asked.

Jim explained how they'd simply traced their license plate number, which he'd gotten. "Anyway," he concluded, "glad it got wrapped up quickly. As soon as you get out of the hospital, you've got to work out where you'll be living, David. Is there anything I can do for you about that?"

"I'll just have to look around. I'm kind of thinking about getting a house. I like the idea of owning my own place."

"That's a good idea. Carrie and I have been looking, too. After all, we'll need more space for the baby."

"You and your wife are expecting?" Pete asked.

"Yeah. It'll be a big change, but one I'm looking forward to."

"Yeah," both Pete and David chorused. Neither could keep the note of longing from their voices.

"You've got time," Jim said. "And last I looked, you had a couple of women really concerned with your health."

David immediately changed the subject to a question about the kind of house Jim and Carrie were looking for.

Jim smiled as he answered his question, but he allowed the change of subject.

LATE IN THE AFTERNOON, Carrie asked Alex, "Are you going to see David tonight?"

"Yes, I'm going after work." Alex had called him after lunch and talked for a few minutes, but she could tell he was sleepy.

"I wanted to come see him this evening. Would that be all right?"

"Of course, Carrie. But by yourself?"

"No, I meant, Jim and me."

"He'd love for you to come. He didn't want me to tell his mother. I think he knew she wouldn't put herself out to come see him."

"That's terrible," Carrie said. "I think you should tell her. At least give her a chance to redeem herself."

"You know, I think you're right. I'll call her right now

and offer to take her to see him." Alex picked up the phone. When her mother answered the phone, she said hello to her but then asked to speak to Aunt June.

"Yes, Alex?" Aunt June said.

"Aunt June, David got hurt yesterday. He's going to be fine, but he's in the hospital. I wanted to offer to take you to see him this evening."

"What happened to him?"

"He was shot."

"That's ridiculous! That doesn't happen."

Alex was trying hard to hold on to her patience. "My point in calling was to offer to take you to see him."

"I don't see why I should go and see him if he's going to get out soon. Just tell him to come see me when he gets out. I have several things I want him to do for me."

Alex sighed inwardly. "All right, Aunt June. Goodbye."

After she hung up, Carrie said, "Don't tell me she refused to go see her son."

"I'm afraid so. But she said he should come see her when he gets out because she has some things she wants him to do for her. Incredible motherly love, isn't it?"

"Oh, poor David. You were right about her. It's so hard to believe."

"What is, honey?" Jim asked, having come into the office as she was talking.

"David's mother doesn't care about going to see him, but she has some things she wants him to do for *her!* She doesn't even care that he's been shot."

Jim frowned. "She can't be that insensitive, can she?"

Alex sent him a grim smile. "You want her phone number?"

"Wow! I didn't believe your description of her earlier."

"Poor David," Carrie said again.

Alex just shook her head. "He knows how she is. He told me not to tell her. But we thought we should give her a chance to redeem herself."

"We?" Jim asked, looking at his wife.

Carrie's cheeks flushed. "Well, I didn't believe any mother could behave like that."

"Do you have to tell David?" Jim asked next. "He's doing okay, but I don't think you should tell him something that might hurt him or depress him."

"It probably wouldn't—he knows what June's like— but I won't tell him. Besides, Carrie says you're both going to see him tonight."

"Uh, I think Vanessa and Rebecca may come, too. Rachel wanted to come, but she's already made one trip up here, and her doctor forbids her to come again."

"Oh, goodness, no. That's not at all necessary." Alex figured David would be completely overwhelmed by so many visitors.

"Does Pete have any family?" Jim asked.

"No, he doesn't. Was he still there when you got to the hospital?"

"Yeah, they're keeping him another day."

"Why?" Alex asked anxiously.

"He was running a fever. The guys said the doctor didn't seem very concerned and said Pete could probably go home in the morning."

"Does David think *he'll* go home in the morning?" Alex asked.

"And where will he go if he does? To his mother's house?" Carrie asked. "I mean, after all, his condo burned to the ground."

It was Alex's turn to feel the heat rise in her cheeks, but she pretended not to notice. "No, he's staying in my second bedroom until he finds a new place."

"He told me he's thinking about buying a house," Jim said.

Alex stared at him.

"Is that a problem?" Jim asked.

"No, of course not. I just hadn't heard that he was looking for a house."

"It may be a sudden idea. You know, what he's gone through can change a guy's way of thinking. I certainly found that in the service."

"I hadn't told anyone that we're looking for a house," Carrie said with a big smile. "That's probably why the subject came up at the hospital."

"Oh, I see. Well, it probably would be a good thing for David to do. It would help with his taxes. And maybe he'll let me help pick out new furniture and decorate it!" She ended with a smile.

"I don't imagine he'd turn down your help, Alex,"

Jim said. "That's going to be a time-consuming project, starting from scratch."

"But it'll really be fun."

"Yes, it would," Carrie agreed.

Jim sent his wife a concerned look. "Do you want us to throw out everything and start over?"

"No, of course not. I love what we have. But if it were necessary, I'd enjoy it. That's what I meant."

"If you buy a house, Carrie, you'll need to buy some new things," Alex said. "You'll have more space and probably more rooms. You'll have to buy things to blend in with what you've got. That'll demand some serious shopping."

Carrie's dreamy smile had Jim sending a look of gratitude to Alex. Then he changed the subject. "How's your case coming, Alex?"

"Pretty well. I need to take the digital camera and get some shots. Then I think I can wrap it up."

"Good job. And quick. We have plenty waiting, so don't think you're going on vacation," Jim told her with a smile.

"With David's problems, I'll probably have used all my first year's vacation days before he's well and in a new place."

"You going to take him home from the hospital tomorrow if he gets discharged?" Jim asked.

"Yes, unless Susan is going to be there to take Pete home. I could give her my key so she could let David in. I might be able to bribe her to go in with him and make sure he gets in bed. But I don't think she'd stay to feed him lunch because she'll want to feed Pete *his* lunch."

"I think you should plan on taking him home, Alex," Carrie said. "Will'll understand that you're not playing around. Especially when we tell him about David's mother."

"I don't want to try his patience too much," Alex said, looking at Jim.

"You won't be. He figured you might need a couple of weeks to finish up your first case, and you've already finished it in five days. One week on the mark, and you'll be ready for another case when you get in here tomorrow."

Will came in just then.

Carrie stopped him to explain Alex's dilemma.

"Of course you should take him home and settle him in. Will he need a lot of care? You could bring him to our house and let Betty fatten him up, if you want. Vivian would love it as much as Betty."

"Oh, no, I wouldn't do that, but if you don't mind, I'll take the middle of the day off, maybe eleven to two, to go get him and settle him in bed, make him some lunch. His mother expects him to do everything for her, but never offers to do anything for him."

"Sure, eleven to two is fine."

"And she's wrapped up the case except for photos,

and I might be able to do those for her in the morning," Jim said.

"I can do them in the morning," Alex protested.

"But then you'd be on the road all day going out to Plano and coming back. If you stay at the hospital with David and then take him home before you come to work, you'd only make your normal drive."

"Good thinking, Jim," Will said. "I think that'll work best. And, Alex, you're doing a good job. Don't worry about the time off to help David."

Chapter Ten

When Alex reached the hospital that afternoon, Susan was already there.

"How are you?" Alex asked, looking first at David and then Pete.

Pete answered at once. "I'm fine. My fever has gone and the nurse says I'm doing well."

"Great," Alex said. Then to David, "Why aren't you saying anything?"

"I'm fine," he said, not looking at her.

She moved to his bedside. "What's wrong?"

"Nothing." Then, as if her concern had opened a door, he continued, "I'm bored to death. It's so unproductive to lie here all day when I need to be at the office."

"Today is Thursday. I bet if you're good, you'll be able to go back to the office on Monday. That's not too bad," Alex said with a smile. "And I think you'll have lots of company tonight."

David looked surprised. "Who?"

"Maybe I shouldn't tell you," Alex teased.

"Come on, Alex, tell me."

"Some of your family are talking about coming."

Susan seemed surprised more than David. "You mean Mom may come? That's a shock."

David frowned.

Alex hurriedly explained. "No, I meant David's other family."

They were interrupted by a nurse's aide bringing in a big bouquet to place on the shelf.

"Oh, how lovely!" Alex exclaimed.

"Yeah, and there're two more," the aide said, heading for the door. "They're on the trolly out here...."

Alex followed her out. "May I help you?"

"That'd be nice. I can only carry one at a time."

They brought in the remaining flower arrangements. After thanking the aide, Alex unpinned the card on the one she'd carried in. Handing it to David, she waited for him to tell her who the flowers were from.

In a low voice, he said, "These are from Will, Vivian and Vanessa."

Susan had taken the card off the largest bouquet. "These are from the people at work. How sweet of them!"

They discovered the other arrangement was from Rachel and J. D. Stanley.

"Rachel wanted to come see you, but the doctor wouldn't let her travel so far again," Alex said.

"Who are they and why can't she travel?" Pete asked.

"She's one of my sisters, one of the twins, and she's pregnant," David said, a smile on his face.

"Where do they live?" Susan wanted to know.

"On a ranch in West Texas," Alex said.

"David, are you still my brother?" Susan asked, concern in her voice.

"Of course I am," he said. "We've been brother and sister for twenty-five years, and that won't change."

"They're not like Mom," Susan said.

"No, and thank goodness you aren't, either. Mom and Janet are in a class by themselves." David smiled at Susan. "Have you told Pete about our wonderful mother and sister?"

"No." Susan avoided looking at Pete and fell silent.

"Who are the other flowers from?" Pete asked.

"My baby sister, Vanessa, and her mother and step-father," David said. "Alex works for him."

"Oh, yeah. But that's not Jim?"

"No, Jim works for Will, too, along with Carrie, his wife."

"Man, your family is growing by leaps and bounds, isn't it?" Pete said with a small laugh. It reminded Alex that Pete was alone in the world.

"Those flowers certainly cheer up the room, don't they?" Alex smiled brightly at David and Pete. "Especially the one from the company. That was so thoughtful of them."

"Yeah," David agreed.

"And I have even better news. I get the entire morning off tomorrow so I can take you home and get you settled in bed, fed some lunch and all that." Alex watched David's face. He hadn't shown much pleasure this afternoon since her arrival.

"I was thinking maybe I should go to a hotel," he said, avoiding her gaze.

"I won't let you do that, David! You wouldn't have anyone there to take care of you!"

"But I shouldn't put you out. It's not your fault my condo burned to the ground."

"No! I'll take you home in the morning. Now, Susan, you want me to get you some supper while I go down and get mine?"

"Um, I'll go with you, if you don't mind."

"Of course not. You guys need anything?"

They both said no and the two young women left the room.

While they waited for the elevator, Alex asked, "What's wrong with David? He seems really down."

"I don't know. He's been like that since I got here. But it *is* pretty depressing not to have a place to go home to, or any belongings." She sighed.

"Well, maybe his visitors will cheer him up."

"Who's coming?"

"I think both his sisters who are in town, and Jim and Carrie. Jim is the oldest of the Barlows, and you'll love Carrie. She's wonderful."

"You mean I'll meet his real sisters? Should I?"

"Why not?"

"I don't know. It just seems weird."

"You'll like them," Alex insisted.

"DAVID, WHAT'S WRONG?" Pete asked, sitting up in his bed.

"Nothing."

Pete shook his head. "Don't tell me nothing when you're acting like the world is ending."

"I don't know. It just seems… My family has never been close," he said. "I mean my adopted family. I guess I was feeling sorry for myself, and now I feel foolish because my real family is making a fuss about me. And then I think about you not having any family, and I feel guilty."

"But I have a really good friend, David. You've stood by me ever since we met our freshman year. Heck, you even shared your attackers with me," Pete said with a grin.

"Yeah, I did, didn't I? And I've also shared my baby sister with you." He chuckled. "She seems pretty much preoccupied with you."

"Is that okay? I've been wanting to ask you, but other things kept getting in the way."

"Pete, I'd love to have you as a brother-in-law, should things between you and Susan work out that way. Compared to my other brother-in-law, Janet's husband, you'd win hands down. I don't know Rebecca's and Rachel's husbands very well yet. They might give you some competition," he added with a small smile.

"Okay. I love winning contests," Pete said with the wide grin that always cheered David up. "And I was afraid that you'd be upset about Susan paying so much attention to me, but I guess the fear was groundless. Especially as you've got Alex hovering over you."

"Now *that* worries me."

"Why?"

"We've never been close. She's independent. And she's always had men around her. Now I've moved into her second bedroom. That seems a little strange."

"Good strange or bad strange?"

"How could it be good strange?"

"Well, if you like being with her, find her attractive, which I think any man alive would, then you should accept what she's offering and see what happens."

David almost jumped off his bed. "Nothing is going to happen!"

"Why are you so sure? You're not really kin to her."

"Yes, I am! She's my cousin. I…I accepted her offer to stay with her because I didn't have anywhere else to go. But I don't think I should stay there."

"Aha! Because it's good strange," Pete concluded.

"You're going to drive me crazy. Don't talk about 'good strange' ever again."

Pete lay back against his pillow. "I don't think I'm the one driving you crazy," he said softly.

"I'm warning you, Pete!"

Alex stared at David as she walked in the door. "What are you warning Pete about?"

"Nothing," David said, scowling.

Alex decided to ignore his response. "Guess what we bought."

"Your dinner," David said.

"There was a bakery across the street. We bought three dozen oatmeal cookies for you to serve your guests this evening. What's left over you two can share. Wasn't that a great idea?"

"I guess so," David said. "I've never played host in a hospital room before."

"Try one, Pete," Susan said. "I don't think one will spoil your appetite."

Pete was willing. Alex looked at David. "Do you want one, or are you going to be difficult?"

"If I don't want to try one, I'm difficult? For all you know, I *hate* oatmeal cookies."

"Do you?"

"No, so I'll take one."

Alex gave him a disgusted look. "Anyway, you're still being difficult."

"Eat your dinner and I'll be nice."

The two women settled down in chairs between the beds so they all could talk.

"I'd be even nicer if you gave me a bite of your hamburger," David said, looking longingly at Alex's dinner.

She immediately offered him half.

"No, honey, I shouldn't even ask for a bite. I know I don't deserve half of your meal. Just a bite."

Alex gave him his bite and a couple of French fries, too. Then she said, "Jim said you're thinking about buying a house."

"Yeah. It sounds good to me after the condo burning down."

"Will you promise to let me help you decorate it?" Alex asked with a smile before a different thought occurred to her. "I mean, unless you—you know—have someone special in mind to, um, move in with you."

"No, Alex, I… I'd really appreciate your help. I don't know much about doing that stuff."

She breathed a sigh of relief. "I'd love doing it. Susan could help me, too."

"It would be fun, David. And we wouldn't make it all stuffy and stiff like Mom's place." Susan's face scrunched up in distaste.

"You're right," David said. "I wouldn't want it furnished like Mom and Aunt Gladys's house. And I like blue, but I don't want it all blue."

"No, of course not," Alex assured him.

The patients' dinner trays were brought in, and David and Pete dug in.

"You know, I don't know how I'll eat alone when I go home," Pete said. "It's a lot more fun to eat with all of you."

"Me, too," Susan said. "I hate eating by myself."

"Maybe we can start having a weekly dinner party, just the four of us," Alex suggested.

"That would be good," David said, "but who's going to cook?"

"Well, I wouldn't mind cooking occasionally, but I think we could go out, too," said Alex.

"I suppose so," David agreed.

They had just finished their meals and cleaned up when their first visitors arrived. Rebecca and Vanessa came in, eager to see David. Susan stared at them, her eyes wide.

"Susan, say hello to David's sisters, Rebecca and Vanessa."

"Hello," she said hesitantly.

"This is Susan, David's sister, uh, other sister," Alex said, suddenly feeling as awkward as Susan.

But Rebecca and Vanessa immediately made Susan feel like part of their family. They asked questions about her life and told her how excited they were to have David back in theirs. Soon Susan was chatting as if she'd known them forever. And she included Pete in her conversation. Then Jim and Carrie arrived. Both David and Pete relaxed a little, glad to have another man in the room.

Alex passed out oatmeal raisin cookies, and suddenly they were having a party. In the midst of it, Will and Vivian arrived.

"Are we interrupting?" Vivian asked with a smile.

David stared at her. "Vivian, Will, we didn't expect…I mean, how nice of you to come."

"Of course, we came. We wanted to be sure you were all right. Such a terrible thing to happen to you, David. And Pete, is it? I haven't met you," she added. "I'm Vivian Greenfield, Will's wife and Vanessa's mother."

The next half hour was enjoyable. Vivian had brought a box of Betty's cupcakes for everyone to enjoy. And she tried to get both men to agree to come to their house the next day to stay until they were ready to go back to work. Both refused but expressed their gratitude.

"I've never had anyone make such a generous offer to me," Pete said.

"Not even your mother?" Vivian asked.

"She died when I was a little boy," he said.

Will grabbed his wife's arm. "Watch out, Pete. You've said the magic words. Vivian will want to adopt you."

Vivian sniffed. "And why not? We have room for him. No one should be without a mother. Is your father nearby?"

Pete sent a desperate look at David.

"Um, Vivian, Pete is afraid to tell you that his father is dead, too."

"Oh, no! Then you have no one?"

"I have David. He's my best friend. And Susan. She's…a friend, too," Pete said.

Vivian patted his shoulder. "Then you're not alone. But we have plenty of room to include you in our family. So I expect you to come to dinner on Sundays with Susan and David. You'll be out of the hospital soon, won't you? Can you make it this Sunday?"

David answered for all three. "Yes, Vivian, we'll be there."

"Oh, good. And you, Alex, of course."

"Are you sure you have room, Vivian?" Alex asked.

"Darling, it doesn't matter if we eat with all of us sitting on the floor. We have room."

"Mom's right," Vanessa echoed. "And it will be nice to have some more women around who aren't married or pregnant!" she finished with a big smile.

Half an hour later, their guests had bade them goodnight. Only the original foursome were there.

"David, your new family is so nice!" Susan exclaimed. "I wouldn't blame you if you forgot all about us."

David reached out his good arm to Susan and pulled her close. "Oh, no, you won't get rid of me that easily, Susan."

She laughed. "Okay, but I feel really sad that our family isn't like them."

David sighed. "You and I are okay, Suse, and we always will be. And I made a promise to Dad about Mom, so I'll take care of her."

Susan hugged him.

"Hey, any way I can get in on the hugging?" Pete asked.

Susan gave a surprised giggle and spun around to the other bed to hug Pete.

"Shoot, and I thought he wanted to hug *me*," David joked.

Alex grinned at David. "I'll hug you, David." She threw her arms around his neck and gave him a hug.

Then she stood. "I think we'd better go and let you two get a good night's sleep. I'll be back in the morning after you have your breakfast to wait for the doctor's decision. Susan, are you planning to come take Pete home?"

"Yes. He's going to call me when he can leave."

"Okay. I'll be here around nine, if that's all right, David?"

"Yeah, that'll be great, Alex. Thanks."

After tidying the room and putting the leftover cookies and cupcakes where the guys could reach them, along with their water pitchers and cups, Alex leaned over and kissed David's cheek as she usually did. "Good night," she called, waving to Pete who had been exchanging soft kisses with Susan.

Susan hurried after Alex.

"Tonight was fun."

"Yes, it was, wasn't it? I told you you'd like his family."

"His *new* family," Susan insisted.

"Actually, his *old* family, Susan. But you don't have to worry. He told you he would always count you as family, didn't he?"

"Yes, but I don't know why he would. Mom is cold and unloving, like always. Daddy was different. He loved both of us. I can't say the same about Janet."

Alex laughed. "No one could say the same about Janet."

"No, I guess not, but maybe she's not as bad as I think she is. Maybe we were all too unwilling to accept each other."

"Susan, by the time you moved to town, Janet was already acting like she controlled the universe, because your mother taught her that. It's your mother's fault that your family isn't a happy one. Not yours."

"You think?"

"Yes, I do. I'll see you tomorrow."

ALEX GOT UP EARLY to prepare David's room for him. She'd washed the sheets the night before and put them in the dryer before she went to sleep. This morning, she had soup cooking on the stove. In addition, she made sandwiches of sliced roast beef and stored them in the refrigerator.

She admitted to herself, while showering, that she shouldn't be so anxious to appear the perfect home-maker to her cousin. But she wanted to prove to him she could make a home. Somehow it seemed impor-tant to her, and she didn't want to think too much about why.

Dressing in a pencil-slim black skirt topped with a pale-blue sweater that showed off her dark-auburn hair,

Alex added the light makeup she usually wore and grabbed her keys and purse. Time to leave for the hospital.

When she got there, she was alarmed to see police cars by the emergency room. Her leisurely stroll was replaced with a jog.

When she reached the front door of the hospital, she was stopped by a policeman.

"I'm sorry, ma'am, but the hospital is shut down for the moment. I'm sure it will open up soon."

"Can you tell me what's wrong? Has anyone been injured?"

"No, ma'am, not at this time. We have a prisoner who escaped. He's somewhere in the hospital. As soon as he's caught, then you can go in and visit whoever you're here to see."

"Please, I'm here to see my cousin. He was shot on Tuesday by one of two men who were quickly found and imprisoned. If one of them is the one who escaped, he could be planning another attempt to kill my cousin."

The officer frowned. "Who's your cousin?"

"David Buford. Could you please check?"

"Just a minute, miss. Sergeant?" the officer called and crossed to another man in uniform.

After a brief conference, the officer returned to Alex's side. "They don't think that was the prisoner who escaped, but my sergeant is going to check to be sure."

"Thank you. I appreciate your assistance."

"You look awfully familiar. Have we met before?"

"No, but I was on the force for about eighteen months," Alex admitted. "I'm Alexandra Buford."

"I'm Butch Erickson."

She smiled briefly, watching for the sergeant to return.

"What are you doing now?" Butch asked. "Did you get married?"

"No, I'm a private investigator."

"Really? Who are you with? Or did you go out on your own?"

"No, I work for Will Greenfield."

"Hey, a guy from his office, Jim Barlow, helped wrap up that mess."

"Yes. There's your sergeant."

"I'm sure your cousin is safe," Butch said before he moved to his sergeant's side.

He came back with a smile on his face. "They caught the guy, but he wasn't the one you were concerned about, anyway."

"Thanks, Butch. May I go in now?"

"Yes, ma'am. Say, here's my card. I'd love it if you'd give me a call sometime. We could go out for dinner and—"

"Thanks, but I'm really busy right now."

She offered him a smile, dropped the card in her purse and headed for the hospital entrance. When she got in the elevator, she tapped her toe, the only anxious expression she allowed. But once she was out of the elevator, she practically ran down the hall and flung open the door, anxious to see that both guys were all right.

The room was empty.

Chapter Eleven

Alex stood staring at the empty beds, panic building in her. She couldn't think of an explanation—except for one she didn't want to think about.

The door opened behind her and she spun around to see David. Without thinking, she threw herself at him, sobbing on his good shoulder.

"Alex? What's wrong? Why are you crying?"

Alex tried to get herself under control. "I…I couldn't g-get in the hospital because a…a prisoner had escaped." At that point her tears grew heavier again. "I thought he'd come to murder you. And when I g-got here, you were g-gone!"

David held her against him, shushing her gently. "I'm fine, honey, I'm fine. They moved me down the hall where several people were gathered for safety. But I knew you'd be coming, so I came back as soon as I could. I'm fine."

She stepped out of his hold. "Yes. Yes, I see. I'm sorry. I didn't mean to…to act like a baby."

"A beautiful baby," he teased.

"Not right now! I've got red eyes and streaked cheeks. Oh—where's Pete? I almost forgot about him."

"Susan got here around eight and the doctor had already released both of us."

"I'm sorry you had to wait. You could've called."

"It was only an hour. I didn't want to rush you."

"Are you ready to go now?"

"Yeah. But I don't have anything to wear but this," he said, stepping back to gesture at his pajama bottoms and hospital gown.

"That's all right. You're just going home. And I bought two pair of pajamas, so you have a clean pair waiting for you."

David put his good arm about Alex's shoulders. "You're the best cousin in the world, Alex. I don't think I've told you that, but it's true."

"Thank you. Let's go home."

"I'm ready."

When they got to the front door, the officer she'd met earlier called out, "Bye, Alexandra."

"Bye, Butch. Thanks for your help."

"An old friend?" David asked as he looked over his shoulder at the man.

"No, but he helped me this morning. He got me some information."

"He looked very interested in you."

Alex gave a chuckle, a relief to her. "Oh, I know. He gave me his card, told me to call him sometime."

"And what did you tell him?"

"That I was too busy right now."

"Huh. So you'll call him when you're not so busy?"

"No, David. I just didn't want to be cruel. He'd been very nice to me."

"I bet," David returned, disgust in his voice.

WHEN THEY GOT BACK to Alex's condo, she'd laid out clean pajamas and a T-shirt for him. If he wanted to take a shower and change, he could do so at his leisure.

David thought a cold shower might be a good idea. When she ran into his arms, crying, he hadn't wanted to let her go. Not a good thought. He grabbed the clean pajamas and closed himself in the bathroom. Then he remembered the doctor's instructions. He opened the door and stuck his head out.

"Hey, Alex?"

"Yes," she answered as she walked into his bedroom.

"Do you have any plastic wrap?"

"Yes, why?"

"I'm supposed to cover my bandage to keep it dry."

"Okay, I'll bring you some."

He'd already figured out she would want to do the wrapping job, so he put his pajama bottoms back on and waited.

"Shall I wrap it around the bandage?" she asked when she returned.

"Sure, go ahead."

She carefully performed the task, then returned to the kitchen.

David got in the shower and enjoyed the hot, steamy spray. When he'd dried off, he put on the clean pajama bottoms and the huge T-shirt, which would easily fit over his bandage. He was glad he didn't have to wear the hospital gown again.

He noticed the big television set that had been wheeled into his room. Nice. He could picture himself lying in bed watching television. That would help pass the time. But where had it come from? Did Alex have a spare?

Once he'd entered the kitchen and sat down at the table, he asked, "Where did the television come from that's in my room now?"

Alex was busy making her own oatmeal-raisin-pecan cookies, so David would have something to snack on. "Oh, I pushed it in there for you. I thought it would entertain you while I'm at work."

"You mean it was in your living room?"

"No, my bedroom. I watch television in bed some nights."

"Then you shouldn't have put it in my room."

"I wanted to. It's no big deal."

"Alex, you're letting me stay with you. There's no need to make any more sacrifices for me."

She stopped what she was doing and stared at him. "You're being silly. Besides, you promised to let me help decorate your house. That's a huge concession."

"No, that's a huge taking advantage of you."

"We'll just have to disagree on that," she said with a big smile.

He gave in and changed the subject. "What are you making?"

"Cookies, so you'll have something if you get hungry before I get home."

"You want me to get fat?"

"No! But I want you to get better. Food, any food, will help."

"I'll remember that."

"Here, I'll turn on the kitchen television for you. You may have guessed by now that I'm addicted."

That's when he noticed a small portable television on the kitchen cabinet. "Ha. No more than I am," he assured her. He discovered reruns of *Magnum P.I.* and settled in to watch. He hardly had to shift his gaze to keep an eye on Alex, too.

An hour later Alex dished up two bowls of tomato basil soup with cheese sprinkled on top. David took a sip of the soup and was immediately won over by her cooking skills. "This is delicious!"

"Thank you. I don't often make it just for myself, but I thought you'd help me eat it."

"Gladly."

A few minutes later, Alex put the roast beef sand-wiches she'd made on plates, and set them on the table. Then she filled a bowl with potato chips and brought it to the table, too.

"I thought the soup was going to be all we were hav-ing," David confessed.

"No, you need protein to get well. I hope I gave you enough roast beef."

"Yeah, this is great."

After they finished eating, Alex started taking the plates to the sink. "Go climb in bed. I'll clean up here before I come in to say goodbye."

"You're sure you have to go?"

With a grin, Alex said, "Yes, you big baby. You're going to take a nap, anyway. You won't even miss me."

"Humpf," he said, and left the room, leaving a smile on Alex's face.

When she went into his room, after knocking on the door, he was in bed, pillows piled up behind him and the television on.

He was lying at an angle, and she took another pil-low to put behind his wounded shoulder. "Is that better?"

"Yeah, thanks."

She bent over to kiss his cheek, but he turned his head and she touched his lips.

Jerking back, she swallowed before she said in a falsely cheerful voice, "Sorry. I'll see you later." And she hurried out of his room.

David watched her go. When he heard the garage door close, he relaxed against the pillows. And thought about their accidental kiss. Her recent habit of kissing his cheek had intrigued him. He'd speculated how a real kiss would feel.

Of course, that brief touching of their lips hadn't actually been a real kiss. He'd seen families who casually kissed one another on the lips. He didn't really think it was a good idea, but then, no one asked him.

Still, he wouldn't mind kissing Alex like that. Only, he'd be tempted to take it beyond a family kiss. And there was his problem. He'd known he had one. He'd just refused to put his finger on it.

He wanted a romantic relationship with Alex.

She, on the other hand, had become more family oriented than he'd ever seen her. Her mother, Gladys, wasn't as cold as June, but she still wasn't a warm person.

Not like Alex.

Alex had never asked his advice or wanted his approval. She'd joined the police force without asking him anything. He hadn't found out about it until she was already three weeks into her training. Then she'd started dating that cop. Susan had told him that. He'd hated the man, sure he wasn't worthy of Alex.

When she'd suddenly changed jobs, Gladys had asked him to check on her new employer. That had been the same day his mother had wanted him to turn plumber to please his sister Janet. It hadn't been a good day. His mood had gone from okay to furious.

After taking Alex to lunch, which he'd enjoyed, he had decided to take control of his situation and back off from his mother. Then he'd been confronted by more family. All he could see at first were more demands on him. And panic about how his adopted mother would try to control his thinking about his new/old family. That afternoon hadn't been one of his finer moments. Lucky for him, they'd forgiven him. And seemed to have inspired Alex about family.

So now what?

He needed to talk to someone. Pete, maybe, but he thought he needed someone with more experience, especially in the heart area.

Jim. Yeah, that was it. David was no longer the big brother with all the answers. Now he had a big brother of his own. He'd kept his cell phone by his bed, and he reached for it.

When he got Jim on the line, he couldn't find the words. "Uh, Jim, I, uh, are you busy?"

"No, not terribly. What's up?"

That was Jim. Straight to the problem.

"I need some advice and I thought you might be able to, you know, help me."

"I'll try. What's the trouble?"

"Um, I thought maybe we could do this in person. But not when Alex is around," he hurriedly added.

"Sure. When would you suggest? On Sunday when you come over for lunch?"

"Yeah, that would be perfect. She won't notice if we disappear for a few minutes...."

"Great. I'll see you Sunday, David. And if anything else comes up that I can do, just let me know."

"Thanks, Jim."

"My pleasure."

"WHAT WAS THAT ABOUT?" Carrie asked.

"That was my baby brother, wanting advice."

Carrie stared at him, waiting for an explanation.

"He didn't tell me the topic for discussion, but I think I can figure it out." He grinned.

"Well, are you going to tell me, or shall I start guessing?"

"It's a beautiful woman, about five-eight, dark-auburn hair, who works for Will."

"Alex? He wants to talk to you about Alex?"

"Good thing she's out of the office, honey, or the secret would be out."

"Sorry, but I'm surprised. I don't see that he's got any reason to complain. After all, she's given him a place to stay and is taking care of him. What more can he... Oh."

"Yeah. I think he's just realized what a wonderful woman Alex is. But how do you go from fond cousin to lover?"

"Yes, that is a problem. Do you have any answers for him?"

"Maybe. I hope I can come up with some by Sunday."

Will came out of his office. "Where's Alex?"

"Out taking those pictures. She wanted to do them herself." Jim smiled, understanding Alex's possessiveness about her case.

Will smiled back. "Sounds like Carrie when you first arrived, doesn't it?"

Jim's grin widened, while Carrie's cheeks flushed.

"Maybe for different reasons," Jim agreed.

"Yeah. She's a nice young woman, as well as smart and beautiful. Maybe I should ask Viv to think about finding a young man for her."

Before Jim could answer, Carrie asked, "Wouldn't Vanessa come first on that list?"

Will looked surprised. "Vanessa? Do you think she's interested in marriage now, before she finishes her degree?"

Jim spoke up. "I think Vivian can concentrate on Vanessa. Alex is already taken, I believe."

"I thought from our initial interview she was dating someone, but I wasn't sure it was serious. And lately, she's always with David."

"No wonder he's a private investigator," Carrie said with a chuckle.

"Why do you say that?" Will asked.

Jim said, "David just called, wanting to talk privately

with me, but he wouldn't say what about. Only that it had to be when Alex wasn't around."

"Ah, I see."

"It won't be an easy transition," Jim pointed out.

"No, but it'll be fun to watch," Will said.

Just then, the door opened and Alex entered, a triumphant look on her face. "I got the pictures I needed. I left the film at the camera store Carrie said we use."

"Good for you, Alex," Will said.

"Do you want to give me another case? I can start on it while I'm waiting for the pictures to be processed."

"I love an eager beaver, honey, but there's only an hour or two until it's time to go home. Why don't you close shop today and go make sure David is doing okay? We'll start with new stuff on Monday."

"But I have to wait and pick up the pictures in an hour," Alex explained.

Jim spoke up. "I can pick them up. It's on our way home, and I'll promise not to open them, if that's what you want."

"I'd rather you look at them and tell me whether I've gotten enough evidence or not. After all, this is my first case. I may have screwed up."

"Okay, it's a deal. Carrie has your number. I'll look at them and give you a call. So you should go on home."

"Okay. But since David's probably asleep, I'll stop at a store and buy him some casual clothes. All he has are the suits that were at the cleaners."

"Good plan, Alex," said Will. "Let us know if you need any help."

Alex opened her mouth, then closed it again.

"What?" Will asked.

"I shouldn't ask, but I'd love if Carrie could come help me shop. Not for a long time, but she's so good at finding things, and we agree in taste."

"If Carrie doesn't mind, I'm okay with it," Will said.

"I'd love to," Carrie said. "Do you mind, Jim?"

"Nope, fine with me. You'll drop Carrie off at our place, Alex?"

"Yes. We can shop at North Park. It's so close."

Will grinned. "I think we should schedule shopping expeditions more often. It seems good for morale."

As she shut down her computer and grabbed her purse, Carrie said, "We'll remember that!"

After they left, Will said, "I'm glad Carrie and Alex are compatible."

"Yeah, especially if she's going to be my sister-in-law."

"Do you think it will happen?"

"Time will tell."

DAVID FELT MUCH BETTER about everything after talking to Jim. So much so that he closed his eyes and slept the entire afternoon. He only awakened when he heard the garage door closing.

"Alex?" he called.

"Yeah, it's me," she called back.

He heard a lot of rustling, but Alex had yet to appear. "Where are you?" he called.

"I'll be right there," she promised.

In a minute she was in his doorway. "Did you have a good day?"

"I guess I slept. The garage door closing woke me up."

"I'm glad you got some rest. Do you want to get up for a while or stay in bed?"

"I want to get up."

"Oh, good. I have some things to show you."

"Um, I have to excuse myself first."

"Oh, of course. I'll be in the kitchen."

When he came in a few minutes later, he found a pile of things on the kitchen table. "This is dinner?"

"No, of course not, but I thought you needed some casual clothes to wear. I may not've chosen what you like, but you need to try them on and tell me what to take back."

"All this? You'd better tell me what I owe you."

"First try them on. The tennis shoes are like the ones you used to wear around, I think."

"Yeah. You've got a good memory."

He went through the pile. There were a couple of pairs of jeans that were the right size, along with shirts. He discovered a warm-up suit that would be easy to wear, some T-shirts that would go with the warm-up suit and the jeans. There was also a great leather jacket.

"This must've cost a bundle!" he exclaimed.

"Maybe, but you can afford it, and Carrie and I

thought it would look very good on you. And it will last forever."

"Okay, I guess I've acquired a wardrobe."

"Good. There's nothing I need to take back?"

"No, I'm pleased."

"Okay. Here's a bag of underwear and socks, too."

"Thanks so much, honey, and let me know what I owe you."

Alex stood. "I'm going to go start a load of clothes."

She started gathering the new clothes in her arms to put in the washing machine.

"You're going to wash all of that? They're brand-new."

"I know, but it's better to wash it and get rid of all the chemicals. Especially the jeans. They're very stiff right now."

"I'm causing you a lot of work," he said.

"I'll let you help me fold them when they're done."

"That's a deal."

"Now, why don't you go back to bed for a while and I'll fix dinner."

"Can't I help?"

"I'm afraid you'll get worn-out before dinner. You haven't been up for a few days and you'll have to build your strength."

"Yeah, but—"

The phone interrupted them.

Alex answered it. "Hi, Jim!"

David stiffened. Was Jim calling to have a discussion with him now? He couldn't talk about it with Alex listening!

"Do you really think so?" Alex said. "Oh, that's great. Thank you so much. And thank Carrie again for helping me shop. She was terrific!"

David waited. But apparently Jim didn't ask to speak to him. Alex said goodbye and hung up the phone.

"He didn't want to talk to me?" David asked.

Alex looked at him, puzzled. "No, he asked about you when I got to work. Should he have asked to speak to you?"

"No! No, I was just surprised."

"I'm sure he's concerned about you. After all, Will gave me the rest of the day off at three-thirty."

"Why didn't you come home then?"

She looked down at the load of clothes in her arms. "How do you think *this* happened, Mr. Buford?"

"Oh, no, sorry, I wasn't thinking," he apologized.

"Besides, if I'd come home early, you wouldn't have had such a nice long nap."

"Yeah, of course."

She left the room to start the laundry. All he could think about was an afternoon nap with Alex in his arms. That would be worth a lot more than clothes.

Something he bet Alex had never thought of.

Chapter Twelve

Alex hurried to the laundry room, grateful to get away from David. She'd suddenly realized how much she'd like to cuddle up with David in bed and watch television…or something. She'd be horribly embarrassed if David realized what she was thinking.

She started the washing machine before she drew a deep breath and relaxed. David couldn't know what she was thinking. It was time to start dinner. She could keep busy, and that was the best plan. Later, after she went to bed, she'd have time to think.

Her last stop on the way home had been the grocery store. She'd remembered what David had said about the meat loaf at the hospital. So she'd purchased some good steaks. She took out her indoor grill and seasoned the steaks before she started cooking them. As soon as the meat hit the grill, she heard David stir.

He came into the kitchen, sniffing the air. "Is that steak I smell?"

"Yes, it is. Interested?"

"I'm beginning to think you're a tease, young lady. You know I love steak."

"I hope you feel that way about vegetables, too," she said innocently.

"I love baked potatoes," he said hopefully.

"I thought asparagus spears would be your favorite," she said in a disappointed fashion.

"Uh, sure, that'll be fine."

The microwave beeped and she opened the door. "Oh, I must've put in potatoes by mistake. I guess we might as well eat them."

"Definitely a tease."

"Why don't you cut them open and put some butter inside. I've made a salad, too. You can put dressing on it."

"Yes, ma'am. What are you going to do?"

"As soon as I turn the steaks, I'm going to go change to jeans and a T-shirt, so I can be comfortable."

He watched her turn the steaks before she ran to her bedroom. He finished the chores she'd assigned him. Then he supervised the steaks. When he thought they were done, he took them off the grill just as Alex came through the door.

"Sorry, it took longer than I thought," she said.

"Must have, since you don't have on any shoes," he said with a grin.

She looked down at her feet and chuckled. "I like running around in stocking feet."

"Me, too. Ready to eat?"

"Yes, I'm starving. Oh! I forgot to set the table." She opened the cabinet and took down dinner plates and opened the drawer to get silverware. Soon they were eating dinner together.

"I had no idea you were such a good cook, Alex."

"My mother taught me. She was determined I'd be a good housewife. I've sorely disappointed her."

"You can still be a good housewife, along with being a private investigator. Look at Carrie. Jim's a lucky man."

"She's a great person, but then, so is Jim."

"Are they having a boy or a girl?"

"I don't think they know yet. But I doubt that it matters, as long as the baby is healthy."

"Yeah."

"I think Will will let Carrie take the baby to work for a while. None of us will mind. She can care for it there and still get work done."

"That's one of the good things about working for a small company."

"I've heard of some places that let employees take their dogs to work."

David sighed. "I'd like to have a dog. We never could as kids because Mom wouldn't allow it. But if I buy a house, I may get a dog."

"What kind?" Alex asked, excitement in her voice.

"I'd like a Labrador retriever, I think. A big dog. But I'll need a good yard because they need a lot of room."

"If I pay half for him, can I be half owner?"

"Maybe."

"Have you thought about where you want to look for a house?"

"Originally I'd thought definitely Plano. But now that I've reunited with my family, I may consider Richardson, a little closer in."

"Are you going to tell your mom about the Barlows?"

"Yeah, I am. I'm just not sure when. I guess when I'm healed. Everything seems so much harder with my wound."

"Is it hurting you tonight?"

"It starts hurting the longer I'm up."

"Then it's time for you to lie down again." Alex got up from the table and took the dishes to the sink. When she turned and saw David trying to help clear the table, she stopped him.

"You need to go lie down. Now. I know you're willing to help, but not tonight. And since we didn't have dessert, I'll bring in a plate of cookies in a few minutes. Find something good to watch on television, and I'll watch it with you. That is, if you don't mind me joining you."

"Thanks, honey," David said, leaning over and kissing her cheek. "I'd love to have you join me." Then he turned and went into his bedroom.

Alex let out her breath. She cleaned the kitchen quickly and then took down a plate and filled it with the cookies she'd made. She made a cup of decaf coffee for David and took it and the cookies into his bedroom.

"Hey, the Dallas Mavericks are playing. It just started. You like them, don't you?"

"Sure, I like basketball." After he'd scooted over in the bed, she handed him his coffee and put down the plate of cookies. Then she turned away.

"Where are you going?" David demanded.

"I'm going to get a soda. I don't like coffee. I'll be right back."

They spent the rest of the evening watching the basketball game, won by the Mavericks. When the game ended, Alex realized David had fallen asleep. He'd long ago finished his coffee. She gathered the plate of what cookies were left and her glass and took them to the kitchen.

Returning to the bedroom, she pulled the covers up over David's shoulders and tiptoed out, refusing to give in to the temptation to kiss him good-night. She turned off the light and went to her bedroom, glad the next day was Saturday.

WHEN DAVID AWOKE the next morning, he couldn't believe he'd slept so late. According to his watch, it was after eleven. He slowly pushed himself up, trying to clear his head. "Alex?"

He heard no response. Getting up, he stumbled into the bathroom. When he came out, he headed for the kitchen to investigate Alex's disappearance.

He found a note on the cabinet by the coffeepot. "David, the coffee's made and you'll find cinnamon buns in the refrigerator. Just put them in the microwave for two minutes. I'll be home around eleven."

He checked his watch again. Eleven-fifteen. Okay, so she was a little late. He got down a cup and poured himself some coffee. After taking a sip, he put his cup on the table and opened the refrigerator door and took out two cinnamon rolls. He put them on a saucer and zapped them in the microwave. Soon he was eating breakfast.

A few minutes later he heard the garage go up. It was amazing how much his attitude improved with Alex's return. He poured himself another cup of coffee and sat down to await her arrival.

Alex came upstairs and entered the kitchen. "Hi, David. How are you doing?"

"Fine." He smiled at her.

"When did you get up?"

"A while ago," he said, deliberately not saying when.

She looked at his plate. Then she picked it up to take to the sink. "You just got up. The plate's still warm."

"I forgot I was facing a private investigator. Excuse me!"

"Did you sleep all right?"

"Yeah, honey, I slept like a rock. You have nothing to worry about."

"Oh, good. I went to the gym and worked out, but I worried about you the entire time."

"I'm a big boy."

"Who's been shot. What do you want to do today?"

"I think Pete and I need to talk and figure out what we need to do."

"The phone's right behind you. Go ahead. I'm going to go take a shower."

"Okay."

"Just don't forget that you promised to go to Vivian's Sunday dinner tomorrow, so you'll need to rest part of the day."

"I just got out of bed," he called after her as she left the room. But he knew she was right. He wanted to conserve his energy. It was important that he get back to the office on Monday.

"PETE? IT'S DAVID. How are you doing?"

"Fine," Pete replied, but David thought he sounded a little strange.

"Did I catch you at a bad time?"

"Uh, kind of," Pete said.

"Hi, David!" he heard a female voice call.

"You have company, Pete?"

Pete sighed. "Just your sister."

"That was Susan? What's she doing there?"

"Uh, David…." Pete began.

"Never mind what I'm doing here," Susan replied, obviously having taken the phone from Pete. "I'm all grown-up and can handle my social life by myself."

"Let me talk to Pete again," David ordered. When his friend got back on the phone, David said, "Sorry I got so nosy. I was surprised. I wanted to know how you're feeling."

"I'm doing better. No fever and only the occasional headache. They told me I should expect that, though."

"Are you getting enough rest? You can tell Susan to go home if she's wearing you out."

"No, she's taking care of me. Knowing we're going to the Greenfields' tomorrow, I thought I should conserve my energy."

"Yeah, me, too. Did you talk to anyone at the office yesterday?"

"I talked to Harry for a few minutes. He said everything was fine, not to worry."

"Okay. You think you'll go in on Monday?"

"I'm planning on it. I'll look a little strange with the bandage on my head, but I figure after the first few minutes, everyone will forget about it."

"Right. I'm planning on going in on Monday, too."

"Good. Do you want us to pick you up tomorrow? Susan has offered to drive all of us."

"I guess I can trust her not to get in a car wreck."

He heard Susan's protest.

"Okay, we'll pick you up at twelve-fifteen."

"All right. We'll be ready."

He hung up the phone and sat there, trying to think about Susan and Pete. He couldn't remember if he'd warned his friend about his mother. He hoped Susan did before things got too serious between the two of them. Or it might crash and burn when Pete met his mother.

Alex came back into the kitchen. "How's Pete?"

"He says he's fine, taking it easy."

"Good," she said as she took down a glass and filled it with water. When she turned around, she saw the frown on David's face. "What's wrong?"

"Nothing!" he exclaimed. When she just stared at him, he said, "Susan was with him."

"That's not a big surprise."

"No, but she needs to tell him about Mom before he meets her. Otherwise, there may be a problem."

"You mean because your mom's a snob?"

"Exactly." He drummed his fingers on the table. "If Susan doesn't warn him, he'll be really angry, and I wouldn't blame him."

"Do you think I should tell her?" Alex asked quietly.

"Yeah. Do you mind talking to her?"

"No, of course not. She may not appreciate it, but I'd feel bad if she didn't warn him about your mother and it ruined what seems to be a wonderful romance."

"You think that's what it is?"

"Yes. At first, I thought she shouldn't fall so hard, since he was her boss, but after seeing them in the hospital, I think they're crazy about each other."

"I want Susan to be happy, but I also want Pete to be

happy. He doesn't have any family. I won't quit being his friend if Susan messes up."

Alex nodded. "Okay, how do you want to spend the afternoon? You'll need to take a nap a little later on. But for now, we can play gin rummy, or some other game, if you want, or you can read or watch television."

"How good are you at gin?" David asked.

"It's funny, isn't it? We've never played before. But I'm better than either of your sisters."

"That's not saying much. Janet has no head for card games at all. Susan is better, but not much."

"Well then, I guess we'll just have to play for you to judge how good I am."

For two hours they played determinedly, each with the intention of winning. When David began to lose, his face showing his weariness, Alex called a halt. "It's time for you to lie down again. Your shoulder is hurting."

"I didn't say it was!"

"You didn't have to. By the way, I won." With a smile she added, "But I'll admit, it's when you got tired that I took the lead."

"That was fun. I had no idea you could play that well."

"We've never spent a lot of time together." She stood. "Come on. I'll straighten your bed for you. Do you need some water to keep by your bedside?"

"Yeah, thanks."

He went into the bathroom while she straightened the covers on his bed and fluffed his pillows.

"It's all ready for you," she announced as he entered the bedroom.

"Thanks. I don't think I'll sleep too long."

"Sleep as long as you need. I've got more laundry to do to keep me occupied."

ALEX ENJOYED HER AFTERNOON, puttering around the apartment, doing chores. She also did some cooking, putting on a pot roast with vegetables and baking a cake, chocolate with white icing. It was so much more enjoyable to cook for someone, rather than simply feed herself. More inspiring.

She found herself humming as she worked. Sometimes, on the weekends, she felt dissatisfied with her life. But not today.

Tomorrow, when they went to the Greenfields', she hoped everything would go well. She'd have to find time to talk to Susan. David had asked her to, and she believed it was important.

But she could admit to herself that it wouldn't have assumed the importance it had if David hadn't asked her to talk to Susan. And that bothered her. As soon as David found a place to live, she was going to have to put some distance between the two of them. She responded to him more than she should.

When he was well. And found somewhere to live.

That could be a long time. With a sigh, she finished icing the cake.

DAVID SLEPT LATE AGAIN the next morning, but Alex woke him up at ten. "I've got your breakfast ready. Come to the kitchen in five minutes."

When he got there, she slid a plate of hotcakes in front of him and passed the butter and syrup.

"Mmm, these look great," David said.

"Good. Here's some sausage, too. Do you want coffee?"

"Of course. I need to wake up."

She sat down with a glass of milk for herself after she'd served David.

"You still drink milk?"

She looked up, startled. "Yes, I do. Don't you?"

"No, I'm an adult."

"I am, too, but milk is still good for you."

He shrugged and then winced. The movement aggravated his shoulder.

They didn't have any more conversation at the table. When breakfast was over, she told him to go take his shower and not to use all the hot water.

She did the dishes and tidied the kitchen before she went to her bedroom. When she heard David's shower turn off, she went into her bathroom to take her shower. It took her half an hour to finish and blow dry her hair. Then she donned a simple but flattering dress. She usually wore pants for her job, and so the biggest sacrifice for her today was the panty hose she had to wear.

When she came out of her bedroom, she found David

sitting at the kitchen table. He was playing solitaire with the cards they'd used to play gin.

"Are you winning?"

"Sure am. Almost done."

"We've got about half an hour before they come. Want to play some more gin?"

"Okay, if you're up to it."

They played cards until they heard a car horn honk. Alex got up to look out the window. "They're here. Guess the game's over."

"And you're happy because you're in the lead." David threw down his hand. "I was going to take the lead with one more card!"

"That's what you think," Alex said with a laugh. "Come on, they're waiting."

"Okay. I hope Susan doesn't drive like a madwoman, though."

"I'm sure she doesn't," Alex protested.

At the car, David opened the back door for Alex and got in after her. "Thanks for picking us up."

"We're happy to pick you up. You know where we're going."

"Good thinking, Susan," David said. He gave her directions.

Pete chatted with David a couple of times, but Alex didn't talk much. She didn't want to distract Susan from her driving.

When they parked in front of the Greenfields'

home, Pete ducked to get a clear view. "I guess they *do* have enough room for us. This place is a mansion."

"It's not like that," David said. "It's a real home. Come on, I'll introduce you to Betty and Peter."

"Who are they?" Susan asked.

"Betty is the housekeeper and Peter is her husband. The two of them take care of the family."

As David got out of the car, he said, "Betty worries about feeding everyone. She makes too much food every time."

"A woman after my own heart," Pete said, getting out of the car.

"We're right on time," David said moments later, leading the way to the front door.

It opened and he introduced Peter to everyone. Then Peter led them down the hall to the morning room. There, they found Will and Vivian, Rebecca and Jeff, and Vanessa, waiting for them.

"Where are Jim and Carrie?" David asked.

"They're on their way," Vivian said. "When you're pregnant, all kinds of things can delay you."

When the doorbell rang, they weren't surprised to see Jim and Carrie come into the room a minute later. Almost at once, Betty came in and announced that dinner was served.

David fell in beside Jim. "When will we get a chance to talk?"

Alex, walking beside Susan, whispered to her, "We need to talk."

Jim whispered to David, "Later."

Susan looked at Alex. "Why?" she asked.

Chapter Thirteen

Dinner was quite enjoyable. Alex was beginning to feel at home in the midst of Will's family, which was amazing to her. As an only child she'd been a loner. But she found this family thing very comfortable. In the past, the only relative she'd been close to was Susan, because they were the same age and in the same class at school.

Susan had complained about her mother and sister constantly. From what Alex heard, if Susan was even halfway honest, she'd suffered a lot. So it was amazing to see such a large family group talking, sharing, laughing and happy. Occasionally, she looked at Pete, Susan and David to see if they were feeling even part of what she was feeling. It was hard to tell, but they seemed content.

When dinner was over, Vivian suggested they go back to the morning room so they could visit. When they got there, Alex noticed that David and Jim were absent. She wondered what they were doing, but it didn't concern her that much. After all, they had a lot of years to make up.

She'd hoped she could talk with Susan sometime this afternoon when Pete wasn't beside her, but that didn't look as if it would be possible. So she turned to her neighbor, Vanessa, and began a conversation. The two of them had a lot in common.

"Do you think anyone will notice we're not there?" David asked. "I don't want to offend Vivian."

"I told Will we needed a couple of minutes alone. What do you want to talk about?"

David stuck his hands in his pockets and turned to walk across the room. Finally he faced Jim. "I…I have certain feelings for Alex. I don't know how to deal with them…or her."

"You mean sexual feelings?" Jim asked, not smiling.

"Yeah. They've kind of taken me by surprise. We've never been all that close until the past couple of weeks. Now I'm living with her! She practically tucks me in at night."

"Have you let her know what you're feeling?"

"No! Do you think I should?"

"Not until you move out of her place. It would be pretty awkward if she wasn't interested but she still had to have you as a guest."

"Yeah, you're right. Maybe I should go to a hotel or something."

"That'll hurt her feelings. Have you looked for a house yet?"

"No."

"Why don't you do that and maybe you can find one you can move into at once."

"That's a good idea. Okay, I'll start looking tomorrow. Do you think it will hurt if I let her go look with me?"

"I think that would be a good idea, because if you work things out, she'd have a house she likes."

"Okay, I can do that."

"Good. Let me know how it's going, okay?"

"Yeah. Thanks for helping me out," David said, sticking out his hand to shake Jim's.

"Did you forget we're brothers?" Jim asked with a laugh, then hugged David. "Makes me feel good that you trusted me enough to ask for help."

"It's nice to have a big brother again, Jim. Thanks."

"Let's go join the family."

IN THE CAR GOING HOME, Pete said several times what an amazing family David had. "You are so lucky, David."

"Yeah, I am," David agreed.

"Too bad *our* family isn't like them," Susan said.

"But now you know the kind of family you want, Susan. When you marry, you can make your own family as nice as theirs," Alex said.

"I agree, if I find the right person." Susan glanced at Pete, sitting beside her, before she looked at the road again.

It reminded Alex of the conversation she needed to have with Susan. She'd ask when to call her before they dropped them off.

When they reached Alex's condo, she waited until she was ready to slide out of the car before she said, "Are you going to be home later, Susan? I thought I'd give you a call."

Susan stiffened. Then she turned around and said, "I'll be at Pete's. Just call me there in a little while." She didn't meet Alex's eyes. "David has his number."

"Okay, I will," Alex agreed, and got out of the car.

"Something wrong?" David asked softly as they watched Susan drive away.

"Do you…I mean, are you aware of how close Pete and Susan are?"

David looked at her in surprise. "What are you saying?"

"I'm not sure. I asked Susan if she'd be home later so I could call her. She said she'd be at Pete's, and said I should call her there."

"Maybe she has plans later that she doesn't want to tell Pete about."

Alex didn't believe that. She was thinking that Susan might already be living with Pete. If so, David's concern and advice wouldn't be a minute too soon. In fact, it would come close to being too late.

"Maybe," she said, and walked to her front door.

Once they were inside, she asked, "Will leftover roast beef make a good sandwich for you later?"

"Sure. And I know I don't need it, but I wouldn't pass up another piece of that cake, either."

"Good. I don't really feel like cooking this evening."

David frowned. "I could take you out to eat. You don't have to cook all the time."

"We've got the leftovers for tonight. Maybe we could go out to eat tomorrow night."

"Sure. That would be great. Do we still have the Sunday paper?"

"Yes, I think so. Why?"

"I'm going to start looking at what's available in housing."

"Oh? Are you in a hurry to move?"

"It's nothing against rooming with you, Alex. But you've been more than generous, and I need to get settled somewhere."

"I see."

"If you don't have anything to do, why don't you help me look?"

"Are you sure you want to involve me in your future? I'll understand if you want to do this by yourself." There was a stiffness in her voice she couldn't hide.

"Sweetheart, what happened to the woman who demanded to help me furnish my house, own part of my dog and help me pick out the house itself?"

Alex could feel her cheeks burning. "I may have overstepped the boundaries. I'm sorry, David."

"I'm not, and don't think you're going to get out of helping me. I need you. You have better taste than me."

"Maybe," she said, grinning, "but if I get too pushy, you need to tell me to butt out."

"Yeah, right," he said, and bent down to plant a kiss on her cheek. "Now, where's the paper? We can divide up the listings and read out loud any that sound possible."

They spent a companionable afternoon. David circled approximately ten houses that he thought might do. "We'll make some appointments to see one each evening. Or maybe two if you think we can tell that quickly."

"I think you can eliminate some of them if the family is still in the house. If you're hoping to rent it until you close, that would be impossible."

"Good point. Thanks, honey."

"You're welcome. Are you ready for supper?"

"Yeah, but let me fix it while you go call Susan. I think she needs to deal with the mom factor real quickly."

"Oh, you're right. I'd forgotten." Alex got up and headed into her bedroom where she'd have a little privacy. When she picked up the receiver, she realized she didn't have Pete's number. "David?" she called.

"Yeah, hon?"

"I don't know Pete's number."

He supplied it and returned to the kitchen.

When Pete answered the phone, she said hello and asked to speak to Susan.

"Hi, Alex," Susan said.

"Hi, Susan. I'll just get right to the point. David and I were talking about you and Pete. He said your mom would have a problem with Pete's last name. Susan, we all know she's a snob. David felt it would be very important for you to talk to Pete honestly about your mom before he meets her."

Defensively Susan said, "I intend to."

"Good. I just didn't want you to forget. It seems sometimes that you and Pete are very happy together. I want it to stay that way."

"Me, too. Thanks, I guess. It won't be easy."

"But I think Pete will understand."

"I hope so. I've got to go. My secret recipe is about to boil over."

"Okay. Good luck."

When Alex returned to the kitchen, she found a pot of tea steeping, the table set and a delicious-looking sandwich at her place.

"Oh, that looks good."

"Thanks. What did Susan say?"

Alex sat down and poured a cup of tea. "She said she knew she needed to talk to Pete, but it wouldn't be easy."

"I agree with that. And I hope she takes care of it."

"It's up to her now, David."

"Are you telling me to butt out? She's my sister!"

"And she's my cousin. But she's also an adult and allowed to make her own decisions. Our job is to support her and help her if she asks for it."

"I think *I'm* the one who should decide if she's capable of making her own decisions."

"And you have to deal with your mother, too. You haven't told her about your family yet."

"I *know* that!"

Alex took a bite of her sandwich and chewed, not speaking.

David did the same, but Alex thought he wasn't comfortable with it. Finally he couldn't hold back. "I'm sorry if I offended you, but I'm older than you. I don't see how you feel you have the right to tell me what to do."

"You know, David, according to Susan, you've been a *great* big brother. But you're not *my* big brother. I'm an adult, too."

Then she stood and carried her plate to the sink. She rinsed it off and put it in the dishwasher. "Feel free to have a piece of cake if you want it. I'm going to read until bedtime."

She left him sitting at the table, his mouth hanging open.

THEIR FIRST ARGUMENT.

It hadn't been a knock-down fight. No, Alex had been very dignified, almost precise telling him that both she and Susan were adults. And she'd walked out before he could make it clear that she couldn't order him around. He was an adult, too, but *he'd* accepted help from his big brother. Nothing wrong with that.

Of course, both Susan and Alex were old enough to make their own decisions. But in a way, Susan wasn't as old as Alex. Her mother—his mother—had tried to make every decision for her and had made fun of her when she'd tried and failed.

So she couldn't really make decisions on her own. That was the only reason he was insisting. He felt quite justified… Suddenly, it occurred to him that she might never learn to make decisions if she wasn't *allowed* to.

He toyed with that idea for a few minutes. Until he finally realized the truth of it and that he'd been wrong. He needed to tell Alex, apologize to her.

He tiptoed to her bedroom. It wasn't too late, only ten-thirty. He rapped softly and waited. He heard nothing. What if she wasn't in there? What if she'd left and he hadn't realized?

Taking a deep breath, he turned the knob and opened the door slightly so he could peek in. Alex was in bed, a book resting on her chest, sound asleep. He'd have to save his apology for in the morning. Crossing the room, he put the book on the lamp table and pulled the covers over her shoulders. Then he tiptoed out of her bedroom and closed the door.

He'd explain over breakfast in the morning.

DAVID AWOKE the next morning with a sense of expectation. Then he remembered his intention to apologize to Alex. He was eager to do so, sure she would accept his apology.

He showered and shaved, then dressed, feeling sure the morning would be so much better because he and Alex wouldn't argue. When he came out of his room, dressed in one of his suits, with shirt and tie, he hurried to the kitchen.

He found a note:

Sorry, but I have to be at work early. Help yourself to whatever you can find for breakfast.
Alex

"Damn!" That wasn't the way he wanted his day to begin. It was only eight o'clock. What time had she left?

He decided to pick up breakfast on the way to the of-fice. Then he remembered he didn't have his car, and even if he did, his shoulder might make the driving dif-ficult. So now what was he going to do?

The phone rang. Hoping it was Alex, he picked it up. "Hello?"

"David, it's Susan. Do you need a ride to work?"

"Yeah, how did you know?"

"Alex called earlier. Did you get breakfast?"

"No, I was going to pick some up on the way in. Can we do that?"

"Sure, if you're ready now."

"Yeah, I'm ready."

"Okay, I'm leaving now. Be there in five minutes."

"I'll be outside."

He grabbed the newspaper he'd marked up yesterday. He hoped to make some calls about houses from work today. Then he went out the front door, locking it as he pulled it closed. Since he had no key, he hoped he could get in when he came home tonight.

He didn't have to wait long for Susan.

She was driving, but Pete was in the front seat beside her.

"You must've gotten an early start, Suse, to pick Pete up and then me."

"I don't mind. Everyone's going to be very happy to see both of you. Oh, and we thought we'd stop at International House of Pancakes. I love to eat there."

"I was afraid I'd spill something on my suit if I ate in the car," Pete added.

"Good point, Pete. Pancakes are fine with me."

When he got to the office, he'd send flowers to Alex's office. With the apology he wanted to deliver.

"DID YOU ENJOY DINNER yesterday?" Carrie asked Alex. They were enjoying a midmorning coffee break.

"Yes, it was wonderful. I find it amazing that so many of you get along. There's no arguing or pouting or criticism. It's incredible."

"Your family isn't that way?"

"Mine wasn't too bad when I was growing up. But

once Mom moved in with Aunt June, it became miserable. Aunt June thinks the world revolves around her. No one else is allowed an opinion. I visit Mom occasionally, but mostly I take her out to lunch, just the two of us."

"Sounds like a good idea," said Carrie. "But our family stems from Vivian's goodness. She knew there were six children that had been separated, and she asked her first husband if they couldn't adopt all of them. But she was very young then and he made all the decisions. He absolutely refused. But as soon as he died, she hired Will to find all of them. She's welcomed each of them as if they were her own children. And me, too. Will had adopted me, more or less. I knew Vanessa, but we'd lost touch. Once Vivian and Will married, they tried to fold me into the family. I resisted, afraid of imposing. But then I married Jim, and I knew they were my family."

Alex gave her a warm smile. "David and I talked about the differences between your family and mine. Then last night, David tried to tell me that Susan had to do things the way *he* thought they should be done. I said Susan was an adult, and she had the right to make her own choices."

"Good for you."

"I guess so. He and I left our argument unresolved. I went to my room and read for a while before I fell asleep."

"You mean you didn't make up with him before you went to bed?"

"We're not married, Carrie, like you and Jim. We're just cousins. Not even that close."

"But David's father was working for your dad?"

"Yes, and after Dad died, June pretended it was her husband's company, even though he had no idea what he was doing. Of course, once David, her son, took over, she was really able to brag."

"That must've been hard for you."

"Not really. Dad and I talked about it before he died. He told me she could say what she wanted. She couldn't take my shares in the company or my mom's shares from us, so we were taken care of."

"That's true. I think—"

The door opened and a delivery boy stood there with a huge bouquet of roses in a green vase. "These are for Ms. Alex Buford. Have I got the right place?"

Alex's mouth fell open. Carrie smiled and said, "You sure have."

Alex tipped him and took the bouquet. He thanked her and left.

She just stared at the beautiful roses.

"There's a card on this side," Carrie said. "I know you've been doing good work, but customers usually don't reward us this way."

Alex set the vase down on her desk and turned to the card. She opened and read the note. Then she cleared her throat. "It's from David."

"Oh. I guess it's personal, isn't it," Carrie said with a grin, clearly giving Alex an out from reading the card.

"I don't mind reading it. He says, 'Sorry about last night. I got my families confused. Yes, you're right and I'm wrong. Susan needs to make her own decisions and suffer the consequences. See you after work.'"

"Well, that was nice of him," Carrie said.

"I guess, if he means it. Some people say what they think you want them to say."

"True, but they seldom say it with expensive flowers."

"Yeah, you're right. I should take him at his word until he's proven wrong."

Will and Jim entered the office just then. When he saw the huge vase of roses, Will looked at Alex and asked, "Did someone die?"

She turned bright red. "No, Will."

"Okay," Will said slowly, waiting for an explanation.

Carrie supplied it. "David sent them to Alex because they had an argument."

"Must've been a whale of an argument," Will said.

Jim smiled at Alex. "It's a nice way to apologize."

Will scratched his head. "Has David got a flower thing? He sent Vivian a bouquet of flowers to say thank you for dinner yesterday."

Chapter Fourteen

Alex immediately came to David's defense. "C'mon, Will. Sending flowers is a nice thing to do. David really appreciates Vivian's graciousness—especially the way she included Pete and Susan. It was an eye-opening experience for all of us. We didn't realize a family could be warm and supportive."

Will smiled. "Sorry. I didn't mean to sound so suspicious of his motives. Of course flowers are a lovely way of sending a message." His brow furrowed. "Were your families so terrible?"

"No, not really. My dad was a good man. My mom is…limited. She feels I've ruined my life because I haven't married and started having babies."

"I'm sorry, Alex, but you do realize she's wrong, don't you?" Will asked.

"Yes, thank you, Will. I actually changed jobs for a man, then realized he wasn't worth spit. But I'm so glad I did take this job. I'm enjoying it immensely."

"Good. Okay, I'm going into my office and getting to work. I'm running a little late today."

After Will had disappeared, Jim said, "We're glad you didn't marry that man."

Alex laughed. "I'm glad, too."

"By the way," Jim began, "what did you and David argue about? Sorry. If I'm being too personal, just say so."

Alex shrugged. "Not at all. David just didn't trust his sister to make the right decisions about Pete."

"And you thought he *should* trust her?"

"Susan hasn't had a lot of experience making decisions, which was his point. But I believe you only learn from actually making decisions and having to live with them. And you don't tell her what to do unless she asks for help. I broke that rule because David said Susan should be told to warn Pete about their mother being a terrible snob. Susan didn't thank me for butting in. But anyway, she's been warned, so now it's up to her."

"But what does her mother being a snob have to do with Pete?" Jim asked.

"Pete's last name is Dansky. His family came from Eastern Europe when he was a child. They definitely missed the *Mayflower.*"

"So her mother will say he's not good enough for her and tell her to get rid of him?"

"She might. I think Susan needs to warn Pete before he meets Aunt June."

"Do you think they're getting serious?" Carrie asked.

"I think she's virtually moved into his apartment."

"But I thought they just met a couple of weeks ago."

"At the most. But since he got shot, she's always with him. And she told me to call her at Pete's place rather than her own."

"And David doesn't know?"

Alex smiled grimly. "He hasn't figured it out yet."

"Didn't you tell him?" Carrie demanded.

"No, because I don't know for sure. I hinted at it, but he didn't grasp what I was trying not to say."

"Oh, dear," Carrie said. "Men can be so dense sometimes."

"Hey, I'm a man." Jim complained.

"Yes, dear, I know," Carrie said, casting him a loving smile and winking at Alex.

WHILE CARRIE AND JIM were at lunch, the phone rang and Alex answered it. "Greenfield and Associates."

"Alex, it's David."

"Yes. Thank you for the lovely flowers. And for the apology."

"You more than earned them for putting up with me. I called because I've got two houses lined up for after work. Can you meet me at 22664 Wind Chime in Richardson at five-thirty?"

"What's the nearest cross street?"

He told her and waited patiently.

After looking it up on Mapsco, she said, "Yes, I think so."

"Good. This house is empty because the couple have already moved away. That's true of the second house, too."

"Okay. So you may have a place to live almost at once."

"Yeah. Okay, I'll see you at five-thirty."

"All right." She hung up the receiver, but her hand rested on it for a few moments. She hadn't believed the day would come when David would buy a house. Which was silly on her part. Of course he couldn't live with her forever.

So why did she feel so unsettled?

"MR. BUFORD, DON'T YOU WANT to go in and start looking at the house?" The real estate agent and David were standing on the sidewalk.

"No, I want to wait for my cousin. She said she'd try to be on time." He kept looking over his shoulder. When he caught sight of her car, he waved to her, a big grin on his face.

When she joined him, she said, "I'm sorry. I ran a little late."

"It's okay." He clasped her hand in his and, with the agent, went up the walk to the front porch of the house. They went inside and the agent began turning on lights and giving her spiel. David listened, but his eyes were on Alex, wanting her reaction to the house.

She said nothing until she'd walked through the entire place, looked in the closets and the backyard. Then
she asked David, "Do you like it?"

"Do you?"

"Not so much. It's a little out-of-date."

"Okay," he said to the agent. "We're ready to see the
other house."

The woman looked from Alex to David and then back
again. "I see. Yes, well, let's do that. I think you'll like it
better. It's only two years old and everything's up to date."

"Great," Alex said.

"How far is it?" David asked.

"Only a couple of blocks."

"Good. Alex, leave your car here and ride with me.
Then we'll come back afterward for your car."

"Oh, David! I didn't even notice you had your car
back. I'm sure you're relieved. But how's your shoulder for driving?"

"Not bad. I just use my left arm more and give thanks
my car isn't standard. Come on." He captured her hand
with his, leaving her no choice.

When they got out at the next house, she turned to
David. "Oh, it's so pretty!"

"Yes, it is, isn't it?"

The lawn was carefully tended, already green in early
March. The bushes were neatly trimmed, flowers
bloomed in the narrow garden, and two tall oak trees
graced the yard.

They walked up the curved sidewalk. The front door was heavy oak with a panel of colored glass. After the agent opened the door, David, holding Alex's hand, stepped inside. They stood in the entryway, admiring the dramatic architectural style of the house. Unlike the last house, everything was new and fresh. The back wall was all windows, looking out on a beautiful backyard.

"How many bedrooms?" David asked.

"There are four bedrooms, one on this level and three upstairs."

"The master is downstairs?" Alex asked hurriedly.

"No, the master bedroom is upstairs."

"Oh, good." Alex responded.

"Why does it matter?" David asked.

"It doesn't now, but if you should marry and have babies, you'd need the baby close to the master bedroom."

"Oh, right."

They saw the dining room and the den, then entered the kitchen. It was a large room with a breakfast bar, as well as room for a table. It had a side-by-side refrigerator and an extra-large range and two ovens.

"Oh, this is wonderful!" Alex enthused.

"You like it?" David asked.

"Don't you?" she responded.

"Yeah, I do."

"Of course, we have to see the upstairs, too," Alex said.

They climbed the stairs. The master bedroom was twice the size of the other bedrooms. The ensuite bathroom had a large Jacuzzi tub that drew a sigh from Alex. "Oh, David, how lovely!"

David had been examining the walk-in shower with interest. "Yeah, it is."

The agent knew when she wasn't needed. "I'll wait downstairs. Take your time."

Alex began opening drawers and cabinets. David turned lights on and off. Then he wandered into the other two bedrooms.

When Alex went into the master bedroom again, David met her there. "I like having a fireplace in here."

"Me, too, but I think it would get more use if you put in gas logs. Then you don't have to worry about carrying up logs or cleaning the ashes out."

"Good point."

"There's plenty of room for a sitting area, a television, some lamps to read by." Alex heaved another sigh. "It would be heavenly."

"Yeah, but it's so big I'm not sure you could hear the baby in here."

"Maybe. But you could get one of those intercoms that lets you hear everything in the baby's room."

"Wow, you've thought of everything, haven't you?"

"No, but I've thought of a few things. Are you thinking of buying it?"

"Yeah, I am. Don't you think I should?"

"Oh, yes, if the price isn't too high."

"Well, let's go ask the agent how much they want."

Again they held hands as they came down the stairs. The agent waited for them.

"Is there anything you want to look at again down here?"

David smiled. "No, I want to know the asking price."

"Well, it's a little high, but I think they'd take less." She named a figure and stood there waiting for David's response.

After a minute David suggested they make an offer of ten thousand dollars less than what they were asking. The agent agreed.

"There's one other thing I want you to ask the seller," David said. "My condo was burned in a fire and I don't really have anywhere to live. So I'd like to rent the house until closing."

"What would you be willing to pay as rent?"

David named a figure that seemed reasonable.

"All right," the agent said. "Hopefully I'll have your answer tomorrow."

David smiled and squeezed Alex's hand.

HALF AN HOUR LATER, they'd picked up Alex's car and were eating in a nearby restaurant. As they waited for the food they'd ordered, Alex said, "I think you made a great choice, David. That house is gorgeous."

"I agree."

"But what if they turn your offer down?"

"Then I'll raise the offer."

"Will you really, David? You really intend to buy this house?"

"Yeah, I do. Are you prepared to help me furnish it?"

"Oh, yes. It'll be so much fun!"

"I hope so, honey."

Over dinner, they discussed the kind of furnishings he wanted to buy. It seemed to Alex that he didn't object to much that she suggested. She suddenly felt concerned that he wasn't making any choices.

"I can't do this if you're not going to tell me what you like, David!"

He looked surprised. "What do you mean?"

"I mean, you're just accepting everything I'm saying! I can't help you if you're not going to tell me what you think."

"Honey, I'll tell you if I don't agree, but so far your choices are everything I like. What's the point of arguing when I agree?"

"You're not just saying that?"

"Nope. I'm working on being a happy family. Isn't that what we learned about a family last Sunday?"

"Yes, but it's not something you can fake."

"I promise I'm not."

"Maybe I'd better wait until I see if you get the house. Otherwise, I'll be so disappointed."

"That's probably a good idea. Let's just eat our dinner."

She said no more about furnishing. But she still thought about how she'd furnish every room.

They went back to her place after they'd dined. Alex checked the answering machine and discovered she had messages. In the first one the feminine voice was sobbing so much, it took several seconds to identify it as Susan's. Alex replayed the message from the start, and Susan's only coherent words were that she was calling from her mother's house.

Alex dialed the number. Her own mother answered. "Mom, it's Alex. Is Susan there?"

"Well, yes, she's here, but I'm not sure June wants you to talk to her."

"Mom, I'm going to talk to her. She left me a message. Can you get her to the phone or should I come over?"

"Oh, no! Please don't. I don't want you and June to get in an argument."

"Then, see if you can get her to the phone."

"What's up?" David asked as Alex waited.

Alex shook her head. At last she heard her cousin's voice. "Susan, what's wrong?"

Immediately Susan started crying again.

"Suse, I can't understand you."

David took the phone from Alex. "Susan, you have to stop crying if we're to help you."

Between sobs Susan moaned, "No one can help me."

"Why are you at Mom's?"

"Because I…I gave up my place and was living with Pete. We came over here so I could introduce him to Mom and she threw a fit and Pete went away and I have no place else to go! Oh, David! It was awful."

"You were living with Pete?" David was clearly in shock.

Alex took the phone back from David. "Where's Pete now?"

"He's…he's gone," Susan sobbed.

"I'll be there in five minutes. Don't worry. We'll work things out."

She hung up the phone, grabbed her keys and purse and headed for the door.

"Where are you going?"

"I'm going to get Susan."

"Why? She's already at Mom's. She can stay there."

"Haven't you learned anything from the Barlows? Family members help each other. You need to go to Pete's. If he's there, get Susan's clothes so she can change clothes and go to work in the morning."

"Damn!" David exclaimed as she left.

It took Alex ten minutes to get to her mother and Aunt June's house, and when the door opened, Aunt June stood there glaring at her. "What are you doing here at this time of the night?"

"It's only a little after eight, Aunt June. I wanted to visit my mother." She didn't dare admit she was there for Susan. She suspected Aunt June would slam the door in her face.

"She's watching television," Aunt June finally said,

grudgingly stepping back and allowing her to enter. With Aunt June following, Alex went to the den, where their large-screen television was located. She greeted her mother, who shushed her because she was interrupting her favorite show.

Alex sat quietly beside her mother. Gladys, her mother, wasn't evil, as she believed her aunt June to be. Gladys was just set in her ways. But there were always commercials.

When the first commercial came on, Alex asked about Susan.

"She's been crying so much June locked her in her room. Good thing. I could hardly hear the television."

"Locked her—" Words failed Alex. Her aunt's cruelty seemed to know no bounds. "Where's Aunt June now?"

"She's watching television in her bedroom. We don't like the same shows on Monday nights."

"Good. Do you have a key to Susan's room?"

"No, of course not. That's one of June's rooms."

"All right. Thanks, Mom." Alex left her mother's side and moved down the hall to the room she guessed Susan must be in. It had been her childhood bedroom. She tapped lightly on the door. "Susan?" she whispered.

"Alex?" Susan whispered in return.

"Can you open the door?"

"No, she locked it."

"Can you open a window?"

"I…I haven't tried. It's cold out."

"My car is parked out front. If you can get out the window, come get in the car and I'll take you to my place."

"Okay, I'll try."

Alex detected hope in her cousin's voice. She tiptoed back down the hall to the front door, opened it and went to her car. Once she'd started it and turned up the heater, she climbed out again and went around the house to the window of Susan's room. She saw the window being raised, could see Susan. She waved and softly called encouragement. After all, it was a bit of a drop to the ground.

Susan shimmied through the window, and Alex helped her down by gripping her around the thighs.

"Come on, let's get out of here," Alex said, hotfooting it to the car. Susan was right behind her.

Once they'd driven off, Alex began giggling.

"What?" Susan asked.

"I never thought I'd be involved in a p-prison break!"

Her laugh was infectious and Susan began laughing, too.

"Me, neither!" After a minute or two, Susan turned serious. "Thank you for coming to my rescue…and not saying 'I told you so.'"

Alex reached over and took her cousin's hand. "We're family, Susan. And you're old enough to make your own decisions."

"And suffer the consequences, I guess."

Alex chuckled. "I guess so."

"The consequence is that Pete doesn't want me anymore."

"Why didn't you warn him about your mom?"

"I thought she'd be better if taken by surprise and presented with a fait accompli—I was already living with Pete. Dumb, huh?"

"Well, it's pretty hard to believe your own mother is as prejudiced as she is."

"David didn't have any problem believing it."

"He's a man. I think they accept things as they see them. Women think they can change things. But I'm afraid Aunt June is a lost cause."

"Yes, I know that now."

"So why did Pete leave?"

"He…he thought I believed the same as Mom because I didn't follow him out. But I wanted to stay to tell her how wonderful Pete is. I thought I could bring her around."

"Oh, Susan. Well, don't worry about it. You can stay with me as long as you want. And you'll get a chance to explain things to Pete."

"I doubt it. He'll probably fire me."

"If he does, maybe David can find you another job in a different department."

She'd reached her place. She hit the button to open the garage and pulled in. Then the two of them went up the stairs.

When they entered the condo, they were both shocked to see Pete sitting at the kitchen table, having a cup of coffee with David.

Chapter Fifteen

"Pete! What are you doing here?" Susan asked with a gasp. Then, before Pete could answer, she covered her face and ran for Alex's bedrooms.

Alex stood there, shocked by Susan's behavior. Then she looked at David and Pete. "Well?"

David spoke. "Pete wanted to know if Susan was okay, so he came here. He thought we'd know."

"You don't hate her?" Alex asked Pete directly.

"No, of course not. I felt bad that I'd left her there. I called to talk to her, but her…mother refused to call her to the phone. Why did she run out just now?"

"I'll go see if Susan will come and talk to us," Alex said with a smile.

When she opened the door to her bedroom, she found Susan sitting on her bed, tears streaming down her face. "Susan, Pete's here because he was concerned about you and felt bad leaving you at your mother's. He even called your mom and asked to talk to you. but she wouldn't let him talk to you."

"He did?" Susan lifted her gaze to Alex's.

"Yes. And he wants to know why you ran past him just now."

"I didn't want him to see I'd been crying."

Alex pulled Susan up from the bed. "Powder your nose and come to the kitchen." She turned to go and then looked back at Susan. "If you're not there in five minutes, I'm coming to drag you out there."

The men stopped talking when Alex came back into the kitchen.

Then David asked, "Where's Susan?"

"She's fixing her face. She didn't want Pete to know she'd been crying. She'll be out in a minute."

"Was her mother mean to her?" Pete asked.

"She locked her in a bedroom and wouldn't let her out."

David frowned. "I should've gone with you."

"Could you have changed her mind?" Alex asked, already knowing the answer.

"Maybe not, but I think I could've shamed her into it."

"You're as delusional as your sister."

"Come on, Alex, I am not!"

"Did Susan say she thought her mother would accept me?" Pete asked.

Susan was at the kitchen door. "Yes. I thought if I surprised her, she would accept you. And I didn't follow you out at once because I thought I could talk her into liking you when I told her how wonderful you are."

Pete stood up and smiled at Susan. "I gather you weren't able to."

"That's right. She adores my sister, Janet's, husband. He sleeps around on Janet, claiming overtime keeps him from home. He's a stockbroker! Overtime, ha!"

"Calm down, honey," Pete said. "It's not your fault. Are you doing all right? She didn't hurt you?" Since he'd opened his arms to her while he asked his questions, Susan told him she was fine. He hugged her tightly to him.

"I thought you hated me!" she exclaimed.

"I was angry at your mother, but I never believed you thought like her. But when you didn't follow me out, I decided you wanted to stay."

"After I tried to argue with her, she forced me into one of the bedrooms and locked the door. I had my cell phone with me and so I called Alex. That was all I knew to do."

"I'm beginning to think," David said to Alex, "that we're sadly in the way."

"They'll just have to tolerate us—it's my place. I'm going to make some hot chocolate. Does anyone else want some? David can tell you about the house he put in an offer for tonight."

"I'll have some chocolate, Alex," Susan said, taking a chair beside Pete's. He sat, too. "David, tell us about your house!"

"Pete and I will stick with coffee. Yeah, I put in an offer for a house. It's wonderful. It has three regular bedrooms and a giant master bedroom."

"Is it two-story or one?" Susan asked.

"Two-story, with a great backyard."

"That's so *we* can buy a big dog," Alex said.

"We?" Pete asked.

"Alex offered to pay for half the dog, so I said she could call it hers, too."

Pete gave David an odd look.

Susan clapped her hands. "Can I chip in, too, and call it my dog, too?"

"I'm sure David won't mind," Alex said with a laugh.

"It's all right, David," Pete said. "We're going to get a dog as soon as I can find us a house."

Pete's words silenced everyone.

Finally David asked, "Are you and Susan planning on a future…together?"

"I am. I hope she is, too."

"Oh, I am," Susan said, leaning over to give Pete a kiss. "And we can have a dog, too? Oh, I love you so much, Pete."

"Yes, but are you planning on marrying? As her brother, I have to ask."

"Yes, of course!" Pete replied, seemingly surprised by David's question. "Why would you think otherwise?"

"Well, the two of you were sleeping together without any mention of marriage."

"Maybe not to you, but that's the reason I went to meet her mom."

"Well, if that didn't scare you away, welcome to the family," David said, extending his hand. Pete got up and shook it with a grin.

Alex stepped forward and kissed Pete's cheek. "Welcome to the family."

"Thanks to both of you."

The four sipped their drinks and chatted companionably for the next thirty minutes or so until Pete said, "Well, I think it's time we let you get to bed. Ready, Susan?"

"Yes," Susan said, clutching his hand as he led her to the door. But before they left, she turned to hug Alex. "You truly are my family, Alex. Without you, I'd still be in my mother's house, believing my life was ruined."

"I'm glad I could be there for you. And maybe one day you'll be there for me, too. That's what family is for."

Susan smiled and nodded. Then she took Pete's hand again and said, "I'm ready."

Alex and David followed them to the door and stood watching as Pete, after a brief kiss, helped Susan into the car and then got in behind the wheel and drove away.

"That was sweet, wasn't it," Alex said sadly.

"Yes, it was. So why do you sound sad?"

"Nothing," Alex said, turning away and closing the door.

David followed her as she went back in the kitchen. Before he could speak, the phone rang. She motioned for him to answer it as she cleaned off the table.

When he did, he discovered his mother on the line. "David? What are you doing at Alex's?"

"I'm living here temporarily because my condo burned down."

"What? You can't do that. You know you're not really related, don't you? I mean, we adopted you!"

"Gee, thanks, Mom, I didn't know."

"Oh, I should've told you. It never occurred to me that you would be attracted to Alex. She's so…so independent."

"Yes, she is. By the way, did I mention my condo burned down?"

"Yes, you did. I'm looking for Susan."

"Why?"

"Because…because I've lost her."

"Haven't you noticed that she has her own place? I believe it's been two years now."

"I tried there. The phone's been disconnected."

"Well, don't worry. I'm sure she's all right."

"Let me talk to Alex."

"She's busy." He didn't want his mother to disturb Alex. "I insist!"

Alex took the phone from David even as he protested. "Hello, Aunt June."

"Bring my daughter back here! I know you took her!"

Calmly, Alex said, "Yes, I did. It was either that or call the police. You see, you're not allowed to hold an adult against his or her will. I thought you would prefer that I just help her out rather than cause a scandal."

"You wouldn't dare!"

"I'm afraid I would. I was a cop, you know."

"Your mother would never forgive you!"

Alex smiled. "I think she would. I'm afraid she'd hardly notice the stir, except that it might interrupt one of her favorite shows."

"Just don't bother to come over here again!"

"I'll be over to see my mother whenever I please. But don't worry. We'll go out."

"Good!" Aunt June declared, and hung up the phone.

"You didn't tell her where Susan is?"

"No, I didn't. When she realized she'd almost been arrested, she forgot all about Susan."

"That was brilliant, honey. We may not hear from her for several weeks."

"Unless her plumbing stops up," Alex said with a smile.

"Yeah. Want to talk?"

"About what?" Alex asked, looking blankly at him.

"About what happened tonight."

"No. It's late and I'm tired. I think I'll just go to bed. You should, too."

David didn't agree, but he went, anyway. They could talk in the morning.

WHEN ALEX AWOKE, she didn't get out of bed at once. In spite of what she'd told David, she had things to think about.

Not about rescuing Susan. She was glad she'd done that. And glad that Susan and Pete had made up. Her problem was David. She loved him. Not as a cousin, but as a man. And he thought of her as his cousin.

What could she do? Here he was living with her, and she wanted him to sleep with her. To have the kind of relationship Susan and Pete had. Would he think she was sick?

They weren't blood related. They hadn't even been raised together. Susan was the only one she'd had much contact with. She heard about David from Susan, but she didn't spend time with him. Only after he took over the company did she get to know him a little.

Then, after she changed jobs, David checked up on her. Likely because her mother had mentioned her worry to Aunt June. With everything that had happened, they were thrown together. And influenced by the Barlows.

But that didn't mean David loved her. They'd become friends. They were going to share the ownership of a dog. They weren't lovers. And she didn't think that would change.

Alex groaned. What could she do?

She shoved back the covers. She'd fretted long enough. Time to get on with life.

After taking a shower and dressing for work, she entered the kitchen. David was there and had made a pot of coffee. She poured herself a cup. "Thanks for making the coffee."

"I couldn't remember if you drank it or not."

"Usually I don't. But this morning I needed it."

"Want to go out for pancakes?" David asked.

"Sorry, I don't have the time." She finished her coffee and set down her cup.

"Alex, I got the impression you were upset last night. Won't you tell me what's wrong?"

"No, David, nothing's wrong. I'll see you this evening. Oh, if you hear back about your offer for the house, call me at work." She hurried down the stairs to her garage.

DAVID STOOD THERE for several minutes after Alex left. Something was wrong. Why wouldn't she talk to him? He was willing to help her with anything. Maybe he should call Jim and see if there was anything upsetting her at work. Yes, that was what he'd do. As soon as he got to work, he'd talk to his brother.

And maybe he'd have good news for Alex. Maybe he could tell her he'd found a place to live and they could shop for that dog they wanted.

His telephone rang at his office a little after ten. The real estate agent had presented his offer to the owners and they'd accepted it. They'd also agreed to rent him the house. However, they insisted on a higher rent.

David agreed immediately. He told the agent he'd

drop by with a deposit for the owners and hoped the closing date would be at least within two months. He'd also pick up the keys.

Before he left, he received another phone call. This one came from the company's contact in the government, letting him know they'd won the contract. That news almost made him forget the other. There were several things that had to be started at once. Their personnel department needed to run an ad for more programmers. And they needed a celebration party for those who'd had a part in preparing the bid.

First he hurried to Pete's office. When he discovered Pete kissing Susan, he came to an abrupt halt and cleared his throat noisily.

"Oh!" Susan cried. "It's my fault, David, not Pete's."

"Okay, I'll fire you instead of Pete."

"No! I don't want to lose my job! You're joking, right, David?"

"Yes, honey, I'm joking. Pete, we got the government contract!"

"We did? Terrific!"

"I also got my house. This is a magical day."

"Oh! I want to see it!" Susan exclaimed.

"I'll give you the address, and you and Pete can meet us there after work." With a big smile, he turned away to leave. Then he remembered what else he wanted to say. "We can have the celebration party at my house, but someone needs to plan it. That might be something good for Susan to do after you see it this afternoon."

"I'd love to! And maybe Alex can help."

"I'd like that, if she wants to." As he turned to go, he added, "Don't call and ask her until after lunch. I want to tell her myself."

And in person. He'd decided to do that while he'd been talking to Susan and Pete. Returning to his office, he picked up the phone and dialed Greenfield and Associates.

He sighed in relief when Jim answered the phone. "Hey, Jim, it's David. Is Alex there?"

"No, David, she's out doing some legwork."

"Do you think she'll be in before lunch?"

"I think she's planning on it. She gave Carrie money to buy her lunch when Carrie gets ours."

"Could you tell Carrie not to buy her any lunch? I'm coming over to take her out. I've got some good news to share with her."

"Sure, I'll be glad to. And after you tell her, maybe you can tell me. I like to hear good news."

"I can tell you now. I know you'll keep my secrets. First of all, I've bought a house, and I'm renting it until the deal closes."

"That's great news! Did Alex see it?"

"Yeah, she went through it with me. The other good news is that we got that government contract, thanks to you and Alex."

"Congratulations. We were glad to help."

"I appreciate it. I'll be there just a little before noon. Keep an eye on Alex for me."

"Will do."

David hung up and headed to the real estate agent's office. He was anxious to get started on filling his house with furniture. And insurance. He needed insurance. He'd just gotten a check for all his belongings two days ago and had deposited it in his account, ready to use it to fill his new house.

After lunch, he would go by his insurance man's office. Maybe he'd better make a list of things he needed to do. He could do that at lunch with Alex.

He couldn't wait to tell her his good news.

ALEX WAS FEELING GOOD when she reached the office. She'd gotten hold of some photos from the fire at David's condo that showed a strange burn pattern. She'd taken them to the fire department and gotten their opinion. Now she needed to talk to Will. If he wasn't there at lunch, she could call him after lunch.

"Alex! You're back early," Carrie exclaimed.

Alex looked around her. "Is that a problem?" she asked.

"No, of course not, silly. You just surprised me. What did you find?"

"Some tracks that indicated the fire had been deliberately set. The firemen didn't see them because it was a night fire followed by a huge five-alarm fire. They checked their records and they never got back out to that site."

"Wow! Good catch, Alex," Jim said.

"Thanks. It made me feel good. So, do you want me to go get lunch, Carrie?"

"Oh! No, that's all right. Jim has already volunteered to go get lunch. I got lunch the last two days, so I think it's his turn."

"Okay. I'll go tomorrow, though. It's been a few days since I went."

She pulled out her chair and settled in, turning on the computer to check for messages.

A few minutes later Alex was busy with her computer, so much so that she didn't look up when the office door opened—until she heard David say, "Hi, Alex."

She jumped. "David! What are you doing here?"

"I came to have lunch with you."

"But Jim was going to get me lunch," she said, desperately looking for him.

"I called him earlier and told him I'd be taking you to lunch. Come on. I have some good news for you."

"Did you get the house?"

"I'm not saying anything until we eat. Come on."

Alex got up and told Carrie she'd be back in an hour. She grabbed her purse and walked to the door with David.

"Are you really not going to tell me until we're eating? Because I think I can guess."

"You think so? Well, I have two surprises for you."

"Two? Oh, my, now I don't know what to think. But I'm praying you got the house. It seems so perfect for you."

He reached over for her hand and squeezed it. "Thanks, honey. I appreciate that."

She smiled at him but didn't say anything else.

They went to the same Italian restaurant they'd gone to that first day, when he'd come to check on her.

"Oh, I like this restaurant," Alex said as David parked the car.

"Me, too." He came around the car as she got out and took her hand in his. Together they walked into the small restaurant. David had made a reservation.

The waiter appeared at their table and offered to bring their drinks while they studied the menu. Alex didn't ask any questions. She knew he'd tell her to figure out what she wanted to eat first. So when the waiter returned with her diet cola, she told him she wanted lasagna. David ordered the same thing.

As soon as the waiter left their table, Alex said, "All right. I've been patient. Now tell me your good news."

"Okay, you're right," David said. "I'll tell you the good news. Which one do you want first?"

She opened her mouth to respond. Then she closed it quickly and smiled over David's shoulder. "Hello, Vivian and Will. How are you?"

The pair had just arrived and, spotting David and Alex, came over to say hello. David said, "Would you like to join us?"

"We'd love to unless you want to be alone," Vivian said.

"No, of course not. We'd love to have company. You can hear David's good news."

Chapter Sixteen

"How nice of you to come all the way over here to have lunch with Alex, David," Vivian said with a smile.

"I have some good news I want to share with her."

Will frowned. "Are you sure you don't mind us being here?"

Since David had changed sides of the booth, joining Alex, he could assure them with perfect honesty that he didn't mind. "Of course not. But you have to put up with my announcements."

Vivian laughed. "No problem."

"Well, first of all, I got the government contract that Alex and Jim helped us with."

"Congratulations, David!" Will said at once.

"David, that's wonderful!" Alex exclaimed. "That's really good news for the company, isn't it?"

"Yes, it is. We're going to hire about ten more programmers."

"So what's the other good news?" Alex asked eagerly.

A grin spread across David's face. "I got the house. They accepted my offer and agreed to let me rent the house until closing." He reached in his pocket and pulled out a set of keys.

"Oh, how exciting!" Alex said, hugging him.

Once more David was grateful to Will and Vivian for putting him on Alex's side of the booth. "Any way you could take the rest of the day off?" he asked.

"Oh, no, sorry, David, but I took time off when you were sick. I can't—"

"How close are you to finishing the case you're on?" Will asked.

"Oh! I got pictures showing a burn pattern that confirms the fire at David's condo was arson. I took them to the fire department and they admitted they didn't get back to that fire because it was a night job and a five-alarm fire occurred a couple of hours later that tied them all up."

"You're serious?" Will said. "That's great, Alex. Well done. Take the afternoon off. You've earned it."

"But I haven't talked to the company," Alex pointed out.

"I'll take care of that, and I'll be sure and tell them you're the one who tracked down the clues."

"That doesn't…I mean, I'm not concerned with getting credit. I just…I've had a lot of time off."

"For good reason. And I think this afternoon might be a good reason, too."

"Yeah, I want to get my house furnished," David

said. "We'll be having the party to celebrate the contract on Friday." He looked at Alex. "You said you'd help me."

"By Friday?" Alex asked in consternation. "David, you can't be serious!"

"Yes, I can. We don't have to finish everything, just the living room and den."

"And the kitchen. Did you think about the kitchen?"

"No, but you can help Susan with the party ideas and just order finger foods."

"How many people will be at the party?"

"Well, we have twenty people who worked on the bid. If they're all there and bring a date, we'll have forty people."

"Vivian, what do you think about renting furniture for the weekend?" Alex asked. "The rental place has some decent furniture, and there's no way to satisfy David's likes and dislikes by Friday."

"With only a few days to prepare for the party, I think you're right," Vivian said.

"Okay. We can visit the rental place this afternoon."

"But I still want you to help me furnish it," David complained.

"And I will, David. I'd love to do that, but not before the party Friday night. That's impossible. What we can try to do is get you some bedroom furniture by then, so you can live there."

"Oh, good."

WHEN THEY LEFT the restaurant, David followed Alex's directions to the rental place. He was amazed at the quality of the furniture. Alex chose a three-part sofa that would fill much of the room. She added several easy chairs in contrasting shades of blue. Then she chose a dining room table with a dozen matching chairs.

"I think that will be enough for the party. Now we need to go to a furniture store and find a bed you'll like, along with the box spring and mattress."

"Good. I look forward to getting my own bed."

"So mine's not any good?" Alex asked.

"No, honey, that's not what I meant. I'm just eager to have my own house again. To own my bed and any other furniture, so if I mess up, I'm the one responsible."

"All right, I won't tease you anymore. Here are the names of several nice furniture stores. Which one do you want to go to first?"

He picked one of the furniture stores and there they found a large bed that David loved. It had a large dresser that went with it and two bedside tables. David bought it all. It could all be delivered tomorrow.

David said nothing until they reached the parking lot. Then he lifted Alex and spun her around. He lowered her back to her feet and kissed her.

Her cheeks turned bright red. David looked at her and apologized at once. "Sorry, I got carried away. You were so perfect, all I could think of was saying thank you."

"That's all right," she said, turning away from him,

afraid of what he might see in her face. "Now we need to buy linens so we'll be ready when your bed arrives. Shall we go to a department store?"

"Yeah, sure," he agreed. They got in the car and he drove them to the closest store. Alex picked up blue linens for the bed. Then she bought blue towels to go in the master bath. "Look at the bed coverlets and see if you find one you like. I'm going to pick up yellow towels for the guest bath."

She hurried off to find yellow towels. When she got back, David had chosen the most expensive coverlet the store offered.

"David, they have less expensive coverlets."

"Don't you like it?"

"Yes, I love it! But I don't want you to spend that much money if you can't afford it."

He leaned over and kissed her lips again. "I promise I can afford it, honey. I have my insurance check."

"Okay," she said, flustered. She turned to the saleslady and let her know they were taking everything, then helped the saleslady package up their purchases.

When they got out of the store, David suggested they go to the house.

"Oh, we can't. I have to go put the sheets in the washing machine."

"I told Susan we would meet them there after work to show them our house."

"I think we can still make it if I take the packaging

off the sheets on the way to my place. Then we can head straight over to your house."

"Okay, I'll hurry."

"But don't get a ticket!"

"I won't, honey," he promised with a wicked grin.

"Behave yourself." She had all the linens ready to go. She carried them into the condo and put them in the washing machine. Once she had it started, she headed back outside where David sat in the car.

"Okay, I'm ready."

"Good, I missed you."

When they reached David's new house, they found Pete and Susan waiting in Pete's car. David and Alex got out of David's car and met the other couple at the front door. After they raved about the beauty of the house, Alex told them about the plans they'd made for the party on Friday and the furniture they'd rented.

David said, "After the party, Alex and I will have time to furnish the place properly."

"But you can't move in until you get some furniture."

"Well, I have bought a bed, and I thought I'd go back to that store and buy some bar stools to use at the breakfast bar."

Alex laughed. "Then you'll only need food."

"Rats! Can we go shopping tonight?" he asked Alex.

"Yes, of course, but we should eat dinner first. I've heard you buy the wrong groceries if you go when you're hungry."

Pete spoke up. "Let us buy you dinner to celebrate your new house."

"That's not necessary, Pete," David protested.

"Yes, it is. And we'll let you buy us dinner when we get married."

"All right. We'll enjoy that," David said with a smile.

They left the house to head for Outback, their favorite steak house. During dinner, they remembered their first meal there, when Susan was trying to catch Pete.

Susan protested, but Pete seemed pleased to know that even then she'd wanted him. "But I'll admit I was a little surprised by you two. I understood Alex was his cousin, not his love interest."

Alex spoke up quickly. "He said I had to come to make the numbers even," she said with a smile.

At the same time David said, "Yeah, we were just learning about each other."

Alex and Pete looked confused. Susan grinned. "I knew it! That's wonderful, David!"

"What is she saying?" Alex asked.

"I'll explain later, honey." David frowned at his cousin.

"Shall we order a Chocolate Thunder from Down Under?" Susan hurriedly asked.

"Good idea, Susan." David waved for the waiter and placed the order. Then he introduced another subject.

When they went home to Alex's condo that evening, Alex hadn't forgotten her question. "What did you mean?"

"She meant she'd figured out why I suggested inviting you."

"To make the numbers even?"

"No, honey, that's just what I told her. And she didn't care what my reason was as long as it got her what she wanted."

"Well, why did you invite me?"

David released a big sigh. He turned around to gaze levelly at Alex. Moving toward her, he reached out to take her hands in his. "What I've been trying to figure out how to tell you."

"Tell me what?"

"That I want you."

He pulled her into his arms and kissed her deeply. Alex felt her head spinning. Her arms went around his neck and she pressed against him. Her blood raced and she didn't bother to think through his explanation, because he was doing exactly what she wanted him to do.

When he swept her up into his arms and carried her to his bed, she gave in to her dreams and urged him on. All reason fled her mind. All she could think of was David.

DAVID PLACED HER on his bed and then lay down beside her. "Oh, Alex, I've been wanting to—" She kissed him, interrupting whatever he'd intended to say. And he had no idea what it had been. She knocked words out of his head. Her silky hair brushed against him, and he ran his fingers through it.

When his skin touched hers, he wanted to kiss every inch of her. But every time he began kissing her skin, she urged him back to her lips and he forgot what he'd intended to do. Then he began removing clothes. When both of them were naked, David whispered her name. "Alex, are you sure?"

"Yes."

When he entered her, he was shocked to discover she was a virgin. "Alex!" he gasped.

"Don't leave me!" she urged.

"No, no, I won't." He held her tightly and began a rocking motion that brought them both to completion. Then they fell asleep in each other's arms.

WHEN HE AWOKE in the morning, David was alone. He got out of bed, finding his clothes all over the room. He hurriedly showered so he could talk to Alex. But when he was dressed and made it to the kitchen, he found only a note. Hoping to read a love note, he got a matter-of-fact reminder about the deliveries to be made today, sitting on top of folded sheets and towels.

He looked at his watch and realized he was late for work. Was Alex at work already? He grabbed the phone and dialed her office number. When Carrie answered, he asked for Alex.

"I'm sorry, David. Alex went out to look at a new case she got this morning."

"When do you expect her to be back?"

"I'm not sure. Shall I ask her to call when she gets back?"

"Yes, please. I'll be at my office until I go to the house to meet the delivery men."

"I'll give her the message," Carrie assured him.

After she hung up the phone, she turned to her husband. "I think I've discovered the reason for Alex's distraction this morning."

"Was Alex distracted? I didn't notice it." Jim was busy with his latest case.

"Of course you didn't. You're a man."

"Whoa, sweetheart. What did I do wrong?"

Carrie shook her head. "Not much. But Alex was…upset this morning and you didn't even notice."

"So what do you think upset her?"

"Your brother, of course."

"What did he do?"

"I don't know. We'll see what she says when I give her David's message."

David called again just before one o'clock. "Has Alex not come in yet?"

"No, David, she hasn't."

"Damn! Oh, sorry, Carrie. Thanks."

"You're welcome, David. Sorry I couldn't help you."

Fifteen minutes later, Alex came into the office, carrying some lunch she'd stopped and bought on the way. "Have you had lunch, Carrie? I can go back out and get you some."

"No, I've already eaten. We thought you'd be back sooner."

Alex avoided her gaze. "Sorry if I took too long."

"No, of course you didn't. But David called. Twice. He seemed anxious to talk to you."

"I don't think he'll be at the office now. I'll talk to him later."

A few minutes later, the phone rang again. "Of course, just a minute." Carrie turned to Alex. "It's your cousin, Susan."

Alex picked up the receiver. "Hello?"

"Hi, Alex," David said.

"David? I thought this was Susan."

"I had Susan ask for you because I didn't think you'd take a call from me."

"I thought you'd be at your new house."

"I am. I'm using Susan's cell phone."

"Did your bedroom furniture arrive?"

"Yeah, it looks great. Are you coming here after work?"

"I don't think I'll be able to."

"When will you be home?"

After a short silence, she said, "I've got some shopping to do. I may not be home until very late. You should go ahead and go to bed."

"I'll wait up."

"Suit yourself," she said, and hung up the phone.

When it rang again, Alex immediately said, "I'm not here, Carrie."

Carrie nodded at Alex even as she answered. "Greenfield and Associates."

"No, David, she left as soon as she hung up. I'm sorry. Do you want to leave a message?"

"No. Just tell her I'll wait up."

"I'll certainly do that."

After she hung up, Carrie turned to Alex. "He said to tell you he'd wait up."

Alex covered her face and groaned.

"Alex, is there something I can do for you?" Carrie asked.

"Yes. You can tell me where the closest hotel is."

"Sure I can tell you that. But why?"

"I'm not going home tonight," Alex announced just as Will and Jim came into the office.

They came to an abrupt stop.

Will asked, "Is something wrong with your place?"

"Uh, yes, there's something wrong with it."

"Then you can stay with us. We have plenty of room," Will said.

His generosity shook Alex. "No, I can't. There's nothing wrong with my place. I just...I need to stay somewhere else tonight."

"Like I said, you'll stay with us." Will nodded, as if it was settled. "I'll call Vivian and tell her we're having company."

Will left the room and Alex stared after him.

Jim looked at Carrie. Then he said, "Alex, is there some way I can help you?"

Alex shook her head.

"You're sure my brother isn't the problem?"

"No, it's not David's fault."

"Why not?"

"I...I led him on." She looked away. Then she turned back to face Jim. "It's because I can't face him that I can't go home tonight. He's going to wait up for me."

"You're sure he didn't do something he shouldn't have?"

"I'm sure, Jim."

Will came out of his office. "Vivian said you should join us for dinner. Betty will serve it at seven."

"Thank you, Will. I have to do some shopping, but I think I can be there by seven."

DAVID WAITED UP until one in the morning. By then he'd given up, realizing Alex wasn't coming home. Because of him.

She probably hated him.

But he'd had no idea she was a virgin. A cop who was a virgin. Somehow, he'd assumed...but he should've asked. He should've taken better care of her. He still had to talk to her, but it wouldn't be here. He'd go to her office and talk there. Where there were no beds. She'd feel more comfortable in an office setting.

He got a couple of hours' sleep. Then he got up early and packed his new wardrobe. He even stripped the sheets, putting them in the washing machine.

As he expected, Alex didn't come home last night or

this morning. He took all his clothing to his new house. He hoped Alex would visit him there. But he had no idea if he'd ever see her again.

It felt good to get some of his belongings in the house. But he wanted Alex there more than anything. When she was beside him, everything seemed easier, happier. He didn't want to live there without her. The dog! That thought pleased him. He'd forgotten his promise to her about the dog. Surely she'd go with him to find a dog.

Then he let out a breath. It was a possibility that she wouldn't. But he'd try. He would definitely try.

After he'd put his things away, he decided to go to Alex's office and ask if he could speak to her.

LAST EVENING had been pleasant for Alex. She'd bought a new nightgown and robe and a new outfit to wear to work the next day.

She'd been welcomed with open arms, including Betty's. Alex figured she'd weigh double her weight if she lived with Vivian and Will. With all that hospitality and good food, she'd thought—hoped—she'd get a good night's sleep.

But no, she hadn't.

She'd had nightmares that had kept her awake half the night. She'd tried to cover the dark circles under her eyes. That didn't work well, either. Betty, having noticed the circles, had tried to feed her more food.

At the office she got right to work, after asking Carrie not to pass on any calls to her unless it was business. She thought that would stop any calls from David. After all, Carrie would recognize his voice.

She'd been working about half an hour when David came into the office.

"Carrie, I'd like to talk to Alex for a couple of minutes in private."

"Yes, of course, David, if Alex…that is, if she wants to. You can use Will's office. He won't be back for a while."

"Alex?" David asked softly, waiting for her answer.

Alex got up from her chair and walked to Will's office without looking at David.

He followed her, carefully closing the door behind him.

"I waited up for you last night."

"I'm sorry. I spent the night at Will's."

"You could've told me you didn't want me there. I could've spent the night at the house."

Alex shook her head. Then she muttered, "It was my fault, not yours."

"Your fault? What do you think you did wrong, sweetheart?"

"I misunderstood."

David took a step toward her, but stopped when she took a step back. "I don't understand."

"I thought you—I didn't understand that you wanted sex."

"What did you think I wanted?" he asked slowly.

"It doesn't matter. Let's just pretend last night, I

mean, two nights ago, didn't happen. You'll move into your house and everything will be okay."

"Are you sure? I don't think I like that idea."

"I think it's the only way to handle it."

"So, as long as I'm not living with you, you'll be glad to help me out? Help me buy furniture, find a dog?"

"I…I will if I have time."

"Alex, this isn't going to work."

"Why not?"

"Because you don't want to be around me. Look, I didn't know you were…inexperienced, sweetheart. I wouldn't have…."

"I didn't want you to know. I didn't realize… I've heard some men don't like an inexperienced lover."

"Is that what the problem is? You're embarrassed?" he asked, his voice rising.

"No! That's not the problem."

"Then damn it, tell me. I can't fix it until I know what went wrong."

"You mean besides my being inexperienced?"

"No, I don't consider that a problem."

"It's too embarrassing," she said abruptly.

This time he stepped forward and she didn't back away. "Sweetheart, I can be patient, but I need to know we've got a chance for a future."

"What kind of future?"

He frowned. "You don't know what kind of future?"

"I don't— You said you wanted me."

"Well, of course, I want you. I hoped you wanted me."

She let her gaze fall to the floor. "I did. But I don't want an affair," she said in a low voice.

"Mercy, sweetheart, I don't want an affair with you, either! I want you to be my wife, to share my bed every night, to have children and a dog. Isn't that what you want?"

"You're not just saying that because it was my first time?"

He stepped forward and pulled her into his arms. "No, I'm saying it because I love you."

"Oh, David!" Alex cried, tears streaming down her cheeks. "Yes, that's what I want, too."

He wiped away the tears with his fingers. "I think we'll be very happy, Alex."

"Yes, I'll be Mrs. Barlow."

"You think so? I have to tell Mom first."

"Yes, you do. I want the Barlow name. I think it's magic."

"You don't think it will hurt Susan?"

With her arms around his neck, she said with a grin, "I don't think so. She'll soon be Mrs. Dansky."

"You're right. I'd forgotten about that. Well, I'll take care of that explanation tonight when I ask your mother for your hand."

"You're really going to do that?"

"I really am."

Epilogue

The Greenfield house was full of family members and a few others who knew the two couples being joined in matrimony today.

Since David and Susan's mother refused to participate in the wedding or accept their choices into the family, she wasn't missed.

The house was full with the five Barlows and their spouses or soon-to-be spouses. Susan was upstairs with Alex, preparing for the wedding. When Susan suddenly jumped up and ran for the bathroom, Alex and Vanessa heard the sound of her throwing up.

"Damn, another one bites the dust," Vanessa said.

"What are you saying?" Alex asked.

"I've seen this before. She's pregnant."

"Really? Are you sure?"

"She'll come out telling us she must have the flu. But she won't have any fever and she doesn't know of anyone who's been sick. Most important of all, she won't meet our gazes."

When Susan returned to the bedroom and told them all the things Vanessa had said, Alex stared at her.

"You're pregnant?"

"No, no, of course not. I just ate something…."

"You're pregnant, Susan, and I think it's wonderful," Alex said, hugging her cousin.

"I thought you'd be mad at me," Susan said with a sob.

"No, honey. I don't think you did it on purpose."

"No one will, Susan," Vanessa said softly. "You're not the first one this has happened to. What does Pete think about it?"

"He doesn't know!" Susan exclaimed with fear in her voice.

"You haven't told him?"

Susan shook her head.

"What happens when you throw up in the mornings?"

"I just wait until he goes downstairs. Then I go throw up."

"Honey, he promised to marry you, didn't he?" Alex asked.

"Yes, but what if he calls off the wedding?" Susan asked tremulously.

"Good heavens. No wonder you're throwing up. I'm going to go get David," Alex said. "Can you stay here with Susan?"

"Sure."

Even though Alex wore her wedding gown, Alex knew David wasn't going to refuse to marry her. And she didn't believe Pete would refuse to marry Susan, either. But Susan was driving herself crazy and probably causing more uneasiness.

When she reached the first floor, Betty came out of the morning room. "Child, what are you doing here? No one's supposed to see you!"

"I need to see both grooms, Betty. It's an emergency. Can you find them and send them to the top of the stairs, please?"

"Okay."

A couple of minutes later, Alex heard heavy footsteps coming up the stairs. Both men, when they became visible, looked worried. When he saw her, David ran to Alex, his arms going around her. "What's wrong, honey?"

"Where's Susan?" Pete demanded, anxiety in his voice.

"I'm fine, David. Pete, um, Susan has a problem she should've told you about. She's afraid you won't want to marry her."

"That's ridiculous!" Pete snapped.

"Have you noticed her throwing up?"

David's eyes widened. Reality hadn't hit Pete yet.

"Well, yes, but I figured it was just nerves. Is she really sick?"

David smacked his friend on the back of his head. "Don't you know how babies happen, Pete?"

It took Pete a few seconds to put it all together. Then light dawned and he stared at Alex. "You mean—you mean Susan's pregnant? We're going to have a baby?"

"Can you promise to marry her, anyway, Pete? She's feeling miserable right now."

"Where is she?" he asked eagerly.

"In here," Alex said, opening the door to the room they were using. "Vanessa, can you come out here?" Alex asked. Then she shoved Pete inside and closed the door.

AN HOUR LATER, two beautiful brides entered the living room, walking together down the center aisle, with the room full of friends and family. Vanessa had preceded them as their only bridesmaid.

A man stood on each side of the minister. When the brides reached the altar, they each took the arm of the man she intended to marry. Vanessa moved from one side to directly behind the two brides, prepared to take their bouquets at the appropriate time.

After a beautiful ceremony, the grooms kissed their brides. Then the minister turned them to face their guests. "Ladies and gentlemen, may I present Mr. and Mrs. Peter Dansky," and everyone clapped. Then he turned to the other couple. "And may I present Mr. and Mrs. David Barlow."

More applause.

Even bigger applause came when Betty announced refreshments were ready in the dining room.

* * * * *

*And don't miss the next captivating episode in
Judy Christenberry's beloved family saga,*
CHILDREN OF TEXAS
*Separated during childhood, the Barlow family
is destined to rediscover one another and
find true love in the Lone Star State.
Look for Vanessa's story, coming in June 2006,
only from Harlequin American Romance!*

American ROMANCE®

A THREE-BOOK SERIES BY
Kaitlyn Rice

Heartland Sisters

To the folks in Augusta, Kansas, the three sisters were the Blume girls—a little pitiable, a bit mysterious and different enough to be feared.

The three sisters may have received an odd upbringing, but there's nothing odd about the affection, esteem and support they have for one another, no matter what crises come their way.

THE RUNAWAY BRIDESMAID

When Isabel Blume catches the bridal bouquet at a friend's wedding, and realizes her long-standing boyfriend has no intention of marrying her, she heads off to spend the summer at a friend's Colorado wilderness camp. There she meets the man whose proposal she really wants to hear. So why does she refuse him?

Available February 2006

Also look for:
THE LATE BLOOMER'S BABY
Available October 2005

THE THIRD DAUGHTER'S WISH
Available June 2006

Available wherever Harlequin books are sold.

A breathtaking novel of
reunion and romance...

THE
F RTUNES
OF TEXAS:
Reunion

Once a Rebel

by Sheri WhiteFeather

Returning home to Red Rock after many
years, psychologist Susan Fortune is reunited
with Ethan Eldridge, a man she hasn't gotten
over in seventeen years. When tragedy and grief
overtake the family, Susan leans on Ethan to
overcome her feelings—and soon realizes that
her life can't be complete without him.

Coming in February

Silhouette®
Where love comes alive™

SHOWCASING...

New York Times bestselling author

JOAN HOHL

HOME TO LOVE

**A classic story about two people
who finally discover great love....**

"Ms. Hohl always creates a vibrant ambiance
to capture our fancy."
—*Romantic Times*

Coming in February.